Stories to Share with My Partner

Book 8

A Northport Booksellers Publication

José F. Nodar

Stories to Share with My Partner Book 8 / José F. Nodar

ISBN: 978-1-7638763-6-1 - Paperback

ISBN: 978-1-7638763-7-8 - E-Book

ISBN: 978-1-7638763-8-5 - Audiobook

Dedication

Foremost, to my wife Miriam, who is always my muse, my inspiration and has made everything wonderful in my life.

Also, to my daughter Anna, and stepdaughters Eliza-beth and Allison, who often give their encouragement and love.

My grandchildren Rachel and David, and my step-granddaughter Andrea, who have contributed to my life intensively without them even knowing it.

To my friends of many years and most recent ones who have tolerated me discussing my ideas too many times at best.

To the talented professionals who have used that talent to make me look good on these pages through their copyediting and proofreading, book cover design, and narration of the audiobook. I am in your debt.

Finally, to my fellow authors, and those who have supported me through my journey as an author. I thank you for your help.

Table of Contents

Personal Ad

Desperate Uncle Seeks Suitable Suitors (Preferably with Excel-lent Medical)

Listen, folks, I'm a man on a mission. I'm trying to launch my two lovely nieces into the world of wedded bliss. They're splendid girls, really. I swear.

Exhibit A (35, going on fabulous): Smart as a whip, successful ca-reer (I won't bore you with the details, but it involves management skills galore and power suits, so you know she's got her life togeth-er). Comes with one (adorable, mostly) pre-teen bonus package (9 years old, loves video games and questioning everything–sounds familiar, right?). Seeking a man who isn't afraid of a little… season-ing. Must be comfortable with the phrase "early bedtime," both his own and hers. Bonus points if you know how to unclog a drain.

Exhibit B (33, and holding strong): Equally smart, equally success-ful (unique skills set, different power suits, but the same impressive bank account). Adores the aforementioned bonus package. Seeking a man who appreciates an excellent wine, a terrible pun, and the occa-sional spontaneous road trip. Must be able to tolerate her sister (see Exhibit A) and me (I'm harmless, I promise... mostly). Double bonus points if you own a Mini. Or a cabin in the woods. Or, hell, even a decent grill.

What they both offer: Enjoyable conversation, excellent cooking skills (they do order takeout often though), and the unwavering love of a slightly overbearing but well-meaning uncle (that's me!).

What I offer: My eternal gratitude, a heartfelt toast at the wedding (I've been practicing), and the promise to stay out of their business (mostly).

What I DON'T offer: Any refunds. This is a final sale.

Serious inquiries only (although a good sense of humour is neces-sary).

Please send photos of your face showing your teeth (just kidding... mostly). Respond with your CV and bank account details and your favourite uncle's joke. If you can make me laugh, you've got a shot.

P.S. If you're independently wealthy and own an exclusive island, please skip the CV and just send the coordinates.

All enquiries should be submitted to springfarm14@gmail.com

The New Recruits

Two aging mafia bosses, Salvatore "Big Sal" Romano and Antonio "Tony" Moretti, are sitting at a corner table at the back of Luigi's restaurant, nursing each a glass of Campari and looking at the menu. They were here before many times and while the food is good, Luigi has not changed the menu in two decades.

Big Sal looks at Tony looking at the menu with a face that brings a smile to Big Sal's face.

"You know what you are having? Right?"

Tony puts his menu down, takes another sip of his Campari, looks at the server, and motions with two fingers for two more.

"Of course I do, pasta Carbona. Luigi does it the best. All these years he has not made a bad one."

The server comes over with the two Campari glasses and they order; two pasta carbonara and a bottle of red wine.

Once the server is out of earshot, Big Sal lets out a big sign and makes a statement: "Tony, I gotta tell ya, I am absolutely miserable.

"Tell me somethin' new Big Sal."

"No, no Tony, I mean it. These new recruits? These kids today? Useless! Weak! It's like I'm runnin' a daycare, not a crime family. Back in the day, a guy wanted to join, he had to prove himself. Now? They show up wearin' sneakers and askin' for mental health days!"

"Don't even get me started, Big Sal. I had one guy last week, Vinny Junior, remind me to whack his father for raisin' him so soft, anyway, he shows up to a job in a hoodie. A hoodie, Sal! Like he's goin' to a damn college lecture, not a shakedown."

"What did you do, Tony?"

Tony looks at Big Sal and just nods his head left and right. "What could I say Big Sal? I said to him: Hey Vinny, where's your suit?"

He says back to me; "Oh, I thought we was keepin' it casual."

Big Sal's mouth is wide open but asks: "And you said what back at him Tony?"

"I said to Vinnie: Yeah? I'm a gonna casually bury ya if you don't start takin' this serious."

Big Sal quickly nods his head: "That's what I'm talkin' about Tony! There's no respect. No work ethic. I got a guy, Mikey Two-Fingers…"

"Wait Big Sal, why is he called Two-Fingers? He missin' some?"

"Nah, nah. He just types really slow. Pecks at the keyboard like a damn pigeon. Anyway, I tell Mikey to rough up a guy who's late on payments, and you know what he does. He DMs him! Sends him a message on Instagram!"

"A message on Instagram? What did he say?

Big Sal's expression is now one of total hopelessness: "He wrote: 'You good?' Like this is some kinda high school drama."

"That's it Big Sal?"

"Yeah. What happened to the days of bustin' some kneecaps?"

Tony responds: "Bustin' kneecaps? Forget that! I had a guy last week, real fresh blood, comes to me askin' about job benefits. He says, 'What's the retirement plan like?' I say, 'The retirement plan is you don't get shot. That's the plan."

"Tony, lemme tell ya, we used to have influence. Power! Back in the day, we owned the city. Do you remember how Vito Corleone ran things? With respect, with fear, with class!

Now? We got kids askin' if we can Venmo their cut. Venmo, Tony!"

"Yeah, Big Sal, we had the cops in our pocket! We had the unions, the politicians, the judges! Nowadays, we got what? A couple of TikTok influencers?"

"You know what Tony I had one of these recruits films a hit for content. Put it online like it's a freakin' tutorial! You imagine the feds callin' me up like, 'Hey, Sal, did you see @MafiaBoi47 just posted himself hijackin' a truck?' What am I supposed to do with that?"

"This is a disgrace, Big Sal! A crime family is supposed to be feared, respected! Now we gotta worry about some idiot leakin' our business 'cause he wants to go viral. I swear, the last real gangster was Jimmy the Ice Pick. That guy didn't even own a phone!"

"The last real gangster? Please, you forgettin' Frankie 'No Neck' Battaglia? That man was built like a refrigerator, never took notes, never left a trail. If you owed Frankie money, you either paid up or you "retired" real early," a smiling Big Sal says as he opened the bottle of red wine.

"Yeah, yeah, but Jimmy the Ice Pick? He took out three guys in one night and still made it home for dinner. His wife never even knew! Now that was discipline. These days, if I tell a guy to take care of someone, he's gotta check his schedule."

"And you know what else, Tony? They talk too much! I got a guy, Joey Likes-to-Chat, tellin' me the other day, 'Big Sal, I think we should have more transparency in the organisation.' Transparency! I say, 'You know what's transparent, Joey? Your skull after I put a bullet through it."

"I don't know, Big Sal, these kids, they wanna negotiate, they wanna 'discuss options.' Do you know what my father taught me? There are two options: do it or don't do it. And if you don't do it, you disappear. Simple!"

Once again nodding and finishing his glass of wine before the pasta arrives, Big Sal adds: "Tony, it's pathetic. We got a fraction of the influence we used to. Do you remember when people feared hearin' our names? Now? I overheard some kid sayin,' 'Oh, that's just Big Sal. He's kinda like a crime influencer now.'

"A crime influencer?! Big Sal, that's it. I can't take it no more. I say we go back to basics. No more applications, no more 'open recruitment.' If a guy wants in, he's gotta prove himself. We gotta weed out the weaklings!"

"You're damn right Tony! Back to the old ways! Toughen 'em up or throw 'em out. No more Mr. Nice Guy!"

"That's right. These Gen Z guys. They call us the boomers."

"Yeah, I give them a boom they will not forget."

"Exactly! Now, c'mon Big Sal. We got to eat and we gotta get back to the office.

"Nah, you go ahead Tony I'll get Luigi to put mine in a takeaway box and I'm calling an Uber."

"A what?"

"My sciatica's actin' up, Tony! Do you expect me to walk six blocks in these loafers? Foggedaboutit."

Tony the Spoon just put his hands on his face and mumbled to himself: "And I wonder why these kids are soft."

Lead The Way

I should have known something was wrong the moment I hoisted the suitcase onto my hotel bed and unzipped it. For one thing, I don't own a floral dress. Or heels. Or an alarming number of hair products that seem capable of either styling or suffocating someone.

This was not my suitcase.

For a moment, I considered the possibility that my suitcase had a secret life. Maybe a split personality, like those characters in movies who wake up in wigs and don't know how they got there. But no, it was simply a case of mistaken luggage. Which meant someone, somewhere, had my suitcase.

My suitcase, which contained my work laptop, three pairs of socks, and, oh dear, my emergency underwear that my mother still insists I carry in case of "unexpected circumstances."

I collapsed onto the bed and groaned.

How had this happened?

My mind raced back in time.

I took the NSW TrainLink XPT train that left Wagga Wagga for Sydney at 1:07 PM, arriving in Sydney at 7:45 PM. As the country train reaches Central station in Sydney, where I had grabbed my bag from the overhead rack in a flurry of people jostling for the exit. I'd been distracted, sure, but had I really taken the wrong suitcase? Apparently, yes.

I took a deep breath and rummaged through the unfamiliar bag for a clue about its owner. A wallet would have been ideal, but I settled for a printed itinerary tucked into the side pocket. "Amelia Parker," it read. The same hotel as mine. Luck was on my side.

With hope in my heart and with a deep concern about the fate of my emergency underwear, I marched down to the hotel lobby reception.

"Excuse me," I say to the receptionist, trying to sound composed. "I think I took the wrong luggage. Would you know if Amelia Parker has checked in?"

The receptionist frowned. "Ms. Parker checked in, but she just left for dinner."

Of course she did. Because fate likes to toy with me.

There was only one thing to do. I had to wait. And while I waited, I had to distract myself from the reality that my suitcase could be anywhere, stuffed in the trunk of a cab, sitting in the middle of a restaurant, or being rifled through by a total stranger who was undoubtedly confused by my lack of hair products and floral dresses.

In the meantime, I did the only reasonable thing: I went to the hotel bar.

Just as I was nursing my second beer and contemplating whether this complete fiasco was a sign from the universe that I should upgrade my wardrobe or go see a therapist to help me get over my fear of flying, the hotel bar door swung open. A woman stormed in, dragging what I recognised instantly as my suitcase.

She spotted me immediately, perhaps because I was the only person staring at her suitcase like it was the Holy Grail, and marched over. "You!" she said, pointing an accusing finger at me.

"Me?" I ask because feigning ignorance is my first line of defence in most situations.

"You stole my suitcase!"

"Borrowed," I corrected. "Accidentally."

She plopped my suitcase onto the floor beside me and crossed her arms. "I was halfway through unpacking when I realised my clothes had mysteriously transformed into this." She gestured toward my suitcase, which, in all fairness, contained a questionable collection of practical yet deeply unexciting clothing choices.

I cleared my throat. "I can explain."

"Oh, I'm dying to hear this."

So, I explained. The train, the rush, the mistaken identity of the luggage. She listened, nodding occasionally, and finally sighed. "Well, at least I know why my suitcase suddenly smelled like Old Spice."

"It is not Old Spice but Red Hibiscus Cologne and you're welcome?"

She laughed. "I suppose it's partly my fault for not checking sooner. Though I will say you travel shockingly light for someone who could be a fugitive on the run."

"Efficiency is key," I say solemnly. "Plus, you never know when you'll need to make a quick getaway."

She smiles, and for the first time, I really looked at her.

She was… well; she was beautiful in the way that made you forget your own name for a second. If I had known our first conversation would involve a suitcase debacle, I might have dressed better. Or at least not had beer foam on my chin.

She reached for her bag and paused. "Wait a minute," she said, rummaging through a side pocket. "Did you… did you use my dry shampoo?"

I panicked. "It was an emergency."

She blinked at me, then burst out laughing. "Well, at least you have good taste in hair products."

"Again, you're welcome."

We stood there for a moment, both grinning like idiots. Finally, she extended a hand. "Amelia."

I shook it. "Ethan."

"Well, Ethan, since we've already done the whole dramatic luggage exchange, do you think you'd like to grab dinner? Since you've already assessed my hair products, we might as well establish if you have equally good taste in food."

I glanced at my suitcase, now safely back in my possession, and then at Amelia, who was waiting for my answer with an amused glint in her eye.

What was the worst that could happen?

I smiled. "Lead the way."

Perfect Fit

Martin Greaves had always prided himself on running the most accommodating funeral home in Northport, New South Wales. After thirty years in the business, he'd developed what he liked to call a "whatever-it-takes" attitude toward customer satisfaction. Still, Mrs Henderson's request that morning had given him pause.

The late Mr. Henderson lay before him on the preparation table, impeccably dressed in what was clearly a custom-tailored black suit that must have cost north of two thousand dollars. The craftsmanship was evident in every stitch, Italian wool, if Martin's experienced eye didn't deceive him.

"Are you sure you wouldn't prefer to keep him in this suit?" Martin asks delicately. "The tailoring is really quite exceptional."

Mrs Henderson, a petite woman with carefully styled silver hair, shook her head firmly. "George always looked his best in blue. It brought out his eyes." She dabbed at her own eyes with a monogrammed handkerchief. "I want him to look his very best, you understand?"

She produced her AMEX Platinum credit card with trembling fingers. "Money is no object, Mr. Greaves. Whatever it costs to get him in a proper blue suit, I'll pay it."

Martin watched her leave, the credit card burning a hole in his pocket. He was still pondering his options when his assistant, Jimmy, wheeled in their next client, a Mr. Peterson from Oak Street, who had passed away that morning.

"Would you look at that?" Jimmy whistled, gesturing to Mr. Peterson's attire. "That's a beautiful blue suit."

Martin moved closer, his professional eye assessing the garment. Pure wool, expertly tailored, with a subtle chalk stripe that spoke of quiet sophistication. And Mr. Peterson was almost exactly Mr. Henderson's size.

The next morning, Mrs Henderson arrived for the private viewing. Martin led her into the chapel with some trepidation, but her gasp was one of delight.

"Oh, Mr. Greaves!" she exclaims, clasping her hands together. "It's perfect! The colour, the fit, George looks absolutely wonderful."

She turned to Martin, her eyes shining. "You must have moved heaven and earth to find such a perfect suit so quickly. Please, how much do I owe you?"

Martin handed back her credit card. "No charge, Mrs Henderson."

"No, I insist! That suit must have cost a fortune."

"Really, ma'am, it didn't cost me anything,"

Martin assured her, allowing himself a small, professional smile. "You see, shortly after you left yesterday, we received another gentleman who was wearing a lovely blue suit. I simply asked his widow if she would mind him being buried in a black suit instead. She said she didn't care what he wore, as long as he looked presentable."

He paused, rather proud of his problem-solving abilities. "So, I just switched their heads."

The silence that followed lasted approximately three seconds before Mrs Henderson's eyes rolled back and she crumpled to the floor in a dead faint.

As Martin rushed to help her, mentally drafting an incident report, he reflected that perhaps sometimes the "whatever-it-takes" approach to customer service could be taken a bit too far. Still, he thought as he fanned Mrs Henderson's pale face with a funeral program, you couldn't deny that both gentlemen looked absolutely splendid in their final presentations.

He just hoped Mrs Peterson wouldn't notice that her husband's head sat a quarter-inch higher on his shoulders than it used to.

The Right Time

D r. Eleanor Carter was not the type to make mistakes, at least, not the kind that involved accidentally warping time and space. Yet, as she stood in her laboratory staring at the blinking vortex of her Quantum Temporal Modulator 6000, she had to admit that something had gone horribly wrong.

She had set out to create a device that could send messages to the past, a noble endeavour in scientific advancement. Instead, she had somehow tethered herself to an infinite loop of the same day, except each time she woke up, it was in a different century. And each time, she found herself entangled with a ridiculously attractive man who seemed intent on making her time-travelling predicament both infuriating and distractingly enjoyable.

Her first stop was in 1745.

Eleanor woke up in a hayloft, the scent of fresh horse manure filling her nostrils. A rugged Scotsman with impossibly broad shoulders and a kilt stood over her. "Lass, ye took quite the fall. Are ye all right?"

Eleanor groaned. "Oh great, I've landed in an Outlander fanfiction."

"Out… lander?" the man repeated, his brow furrowing.

"Never mind. Who are you?"

"I am Lachlan McGregor, at your service." He flashed a grin that could convince a nun to give up her vows. "And who might ye be, appearing out of nowhere like a fairy spirit?"

Eleanor considered the pros and cons of explaining quantum physics to an 18th-century man in a kilt and then decided against it. "Just… passing through."

One heated barn-side flirtation later, Eleanor was yanked back into the vortex and woke up in 1893, this time in a lavish parlour.

A sharply dressed gentleman with spectacles and an impressive moustache regarded her with polite curiosity. "Madam, I do not believe we have been introduced."

"That would be because I just fell through a hole in time and landed in your Victorian sitting room," Eleanor muttered.

"Ah," he said, as if that were a perfectly reasonable response. "I am Theodore Winchester, inventor. And you are?"

"In so much trouble," she groaned.

By the time she reached the 1920s, Eleanor had stopped questioning the sheer absurdity of her situation. She was now in a jazz club, staring at a roguishly handsome saxophonist named Jack. He smirked at her. "You look lost, doll. Want a drink?"

"I want my lab back," she huffed.

"Not much of a drinker, huh? That's all right. I like a lady with a clear head."

He offered a slow grin, and Eleanor felt her resolve wobble. Oh no, not again.

Centuries blurred by in a series of ridiculous, romantic entanglements. After the saxophonist came the swashbuckling pirate who wanted to kidnap her and hold her for ramson followed by the brooding painter who insists she sit for a nude portrait and then came the American cowboy who called her "ma'am" in a way that made her knees weak.

But the loop never stopped.

No matter what she did and how far in a relationship she went, she kept jumping from timeline to timeline.

From the arms of a chivalrous knight or a 1980s rockstar, the vortex would pull her away, flinging her into another time.

Back and forth.

Back and forth.

And then, finally, she landed in 3025.

This time, she woke up in what looked like a futuristic cityscape, neon lights reflecting off gleaming metal buildings. A man in a sleek uniform stared down at her, his silver eyes flashing with curiosity.

"Fascinating," he murmurs. "Temporal displacement?"

Eleanor gasped. "Oh, thank God! Someone who actually understands what's happening! Please tell me you can fix this."

He extended a hand to help her up. "Captain Orion Valen, at your service. And yes, Dr. Carter, I believe I can help you. But first care for a drink?"

Eleanor sighs, running a hand through her dishevelled hair. "You know what? Fine. But if this is another flirtation, I swear on every scientific principle in the universe…"

He chuckles. "Relax, Doctor. In this century, we believe in fixing problems first. Flirting comes second."

For the first time in what felt like an eternity, Eleanor smiled. Just maybe, she had finally landed at the right time.

22

The Pickpocket's Diary

Carlo 'The Pick' Moretti had always prided himself on his light fingers and quick feet. As a pickpocket, he considered himself an artist, a master of the gentle lift, the whisper-thin touch that relieved tourists and businessmen of their wallets, watches, and occasionally, their dignity. He had never been caught. Never.

Having practise his trade in New York city, Carlo had accumulated a bit of funds and decided that a change of scenery, maybe a brief holiday in Rome, Italy, might be good for him.

So, he packed his one bag, bought a flight from New York, and landed in Rome, the eternal city, and boy was Carlo in for a treat.

After checking in and taking a nap, Carlo went out for a drink and take on the scenery of the city, but old habits die hard and soon he spotted a mark.

It had been a normal early evening in Rome, the cobblestone streets packed with couples going out oblivious to their surroundings and Carlo spotted his mark, a tall, well-dressed man in a tailored suit, his leather wallet practically begging to be plucked. A quick bump, a nimble flick of the wrist, and the wallet was his.

Easy.

Or so he thought.

Carlo quickly headed into the nearest restaurant, ordered some wine and a pizza, and looked at what he had lifted from the man.

Quickly, Carlo realised he had picked the wrong pocket.

Carlo flipped the wallet open, expecting the usual: a credit card, some cash, maybe even a lucky lotto ticket. Instead, he found a small, leather-bound notebook. Curiosity got the better of him, and he flipped to the first page.

It was a diary.

A diary with an extremely detailed plan in English to assassinate the Pope.

Carlo blinked. He read it again. He blinked some more.

"Oh, damn," he muttered.

Flipping through the pages, he saw blueprints of Vatican City, many security details, and notes about the Pope's schedule. Every page was covered in disturbingly neat handwriting, outlining a highly plausible assassination plot.

"Crap, crap, crap," Carlo says aloud. "He does not look American, European maybe, and the wallet contained just a few hundred euros and this little notebook. Nothing else. Not even a driver's license or an ID."

Normally, he would toss the wallet somewhere and walk away, but this time, he was intrigued.

This was a once-in-a-lifetime crime-in-progress scenario, and Carlo had never been one to back away from an adventure.

Also, it was probably bad karma to let the Pope get assassinated.

So, for the first time in his illustrious career, Carlo got involved.

His first step was to tail the original owner of the diary. That was easier said than done because the guy was not just some fancy businessman but an assassin. This meant Carlo had to be extra sneaky, which was easy, considering he had spent most of his life in New York city sneaking around stealing things.

He found a hotel passkey with a name and went there and as he reached the hotel; he could see the Vatican and there, sitting in a café, was the assassin.

The man was sipping an espresso like a villain in a spy movie, completely unaware that a petty thief had pilfered his murder plans.

Carlo needed help.

Preferably from someone who knew how to stop assassinations.

He briefly considered the police. Then he remembered he had about seventeen outstanding warrants across three counties back in New York.

"Right, that will not work. Next idea," he muttered to himself.

Then it hit him: the Swiss Guard.

Carlo returns to his hotel to change clothes and on his way back to the Vatican he skilfully lifts some credentials from an unsuspecting dignitary who was a journalist.

Now Carlo finds himself inside and he tries to desperately get the attention of one of the Swiss Guards, who were more focused on looking intimidating than listening to him.

"Hey! Buddy! You guys might wanna know that there's a whole thing happening, an assassination, very dramatic, a terrible scene, dude."

The guard squinted at him. "Do you have an appointment?"

"No, but I have this," Carlo says, shoving the diary forward.

The guard took one look at it and frowned. "Where did you get this?"

Carlo hesitated. "Uh…a friend gave it to me?"

"And who is this friend?"

"You know, a friend, actually a friend of a friend. Very private guy. Does a lot of reading."

The guard rolled his eyes. "Sir, if this is some kind of joke?"

Before he could finish his sentence, there was a loud explosion in the distance.

Carlo gulped. "Okaaaay, I think we just ran out of time for the small talk."

The assassin's plan was absurdly over-the-top.

A distraction in the square, a drone carrying explosives, and a backup sniper hiding in the bell tower of St. Peter's Basilica.

It was ridiculous.

It was elaborate.

It was going to work.

Unless Carlo did something even more ridiculous.

The first thing he did was what he did best; pick pocketing.

He sprinted toward the crowd, relieved a few tourists of their sunglasses, hats, and, most importantly, a police officer's gun.

He had no intention of using it. He had never even handled one before, but Carlo had watched a lot of Hollywood movies and knew that waving a gun around made people listen.

"EVERYONE FREEZE!" he yells, waving the gun in the air.

Naturally, everyone panicked and screamed, which was not ideal.

"WAIT! WAIT! No one is getting shot!" he tried to clarify. "This is just a distraction! A GOOD distraction!"

That didn't help.

Meanwhile, the drone was getting closer to its target. Thinking quickly, Carlo grabbed a bread stick from a nearby market stall, took careful aim, and hurled it at the drone.

As luck would have it, the bread stick hit the drone.

The drone wobbled, veered off course, and crashed into a statue, its payload of explosives detonating harmlessly into it.

"Holy crap. That actually worked," he muttered.

The crowd was now in total chaos, and Carlo used the distraction to sprint toward the bell tower and raised up the stairs where the backup sniper was setting up. Unfortunately, the sniper was significantly more prepared than Carlo was.

"Not good, not good, not good," Carlo mutters as he ran, dodging bullets and regretting every life decision that had led to this moment.

Thinking fast, he did the only thing that made sense.

He threw the gun he had stolen at the sniper's head.

The man ducked, confused. "Hast du gerade eine Waffe auf mich geworfen?"

"Yeah. Same to you, buddy. I got no idea what you just said." Carlo panted.

Before the sniper could recover, Carlo tackled him, and they both tumbled down the stairs. The fight ended with Carlo on top, pinning the assassin down with all the strength his street-hustler muscles could muster.

At that moment, the Swiss Guard, and the Carabinieri finally showed up.

In the aftermath, Carlo was taken into custody, but instead of being thrown into a dungeon, he found himself in a fancy Vatican office.

A familiar old man in white robes sat across from him, smiling.

"So, you saved my life with a breadstick and reckless stupidity," says the Pope with his Argentine accent easily heard.

Carlo shrugged. "Yes, I guess I did, your highness."

The Pope laughed and nodded. "Would you like a job?"

Carlo blinked. "Like… as a pickpocket consultant?"

"No," the Pope chuckles. "Security. If you can outthink an assassin, I think you'd be quite useful."

Carlo considered it.

A stable job.

No running from the cops.

And maybe, just maybe, a little divine forgiveness for his past sins.

"Alright, Your highness. This might be good for me, but I have some baggage, if you know what I mean."

"I know my son. I know people too in New York city. It will be taken care of."

"Great then. It is a deal." Carlo says, shaking his hand.

And that was how Carlo 'The Pick' Moretti became the most unconventional member of the Pope's security team in Vatican history.

Love In The Margins

Walking into the old bookshop, the first thing Miriam noticed was the smell of the old and new books and the faintest trace of roasted coffee from the café next door as the door opened each time a customer walked in or out of the shop.

Miriam loved it here. She was not an enthusiastic fan of reading, but every so often a delightful book would find its way into her home, and she would devour it. Since moving to Northport, besides her home, this shop had become her haven, the one place in Northport where she felt utterly at peace after her divorce.

José. F. Nodar, the bookshop's new owner and local author, gave her a friendly nod from behind the counter. "Back again?" he teases, wiping his hands on a cloth before resuming his careful organisation of a pile of newly arrived paperbacks.

"Couldn't stay away if I tried," Miriam admitted with a grin.

She had moved to Northport only six months ago, seeking refuge from the chaos of the inner suburbs of Leichhardt in Sydney, and the old bookshop had quickly become her second home.

Glancing around the shop bookshelves, her eyes caught a worn copy of Persuasion by Jane Austen. She remembered reading it many years ago and somehow her copy was lost in the many moves she had done over the years during her marriage. She picked the book up and as Miriam flipped through the pages, a small piece of folded paper slipped from between the chapters and floated to the floor.

Curious, Miriam bent down to pick it up. The handwriting was elegant but slightly hurried, as though the writer had been caught between thought and impulse.

"If you love stories, perhaps you love mysteries, too. If you wish to play, your first clue awaits you where stories take flight."

"Whoa," Miriam mutters softly to herself. "What is this? A scavenger hunt? "

Who had left this note? And why?

She looked up at José, but he was lost in his task, oblivious to her discovery. She glanced around the store. There were a few customers, but no one was watching her.

Excitement bubbled up in her chest.

She hadn't felt a thrill like this in ages, not since her divorce.

"Where stories take flight…" she murmurs, thinking.

Then it hit her. The children's section.

Stories were the wings of imagination, weren't they?

Without hesitation, she made her way to the back of the shop, where colourful covers beckoned young readers.

She scanned the shelves until her eyes landed on a copy of Peter Pan. Something about it called to her. She pulled it free, and sure enough, another slip of paper fluttered to the floor.

"Second star to the right and straight on till morning… or just head to the place where pages are set free."

Miriam grinned.

This mystery person had a flair for literary clues.

She knew exactly where to go next, the town's Little Free Library, a charming wooden box on the corner of John Street and Argyle Street where the old bank used to be, where residents left books for others to borrow.

Stuffing the note into her pocket, she waved a quick goodbye to José and stepped out onto the bustling streets of Northport.

The afternoon sun warmed her skin as she made her way toward the corner.

The Little Free Library was on the side of the old bank building behind the bus stop with its own little bench. Miriam smiled as she looked up at the large jacaranda tree, its purple blossoms carpeting the ground.

She opened the box, rifled through the books, and looked like a madwoman digging for gold. A few couples saw her and walked past her with some interesting looks, but Miriam did not care, and then she found it.

Tucked between a well-worn copy of The Great Gatsby and a tattered travel guide to Italy was another note.

"Sometimes, the best stories are written in foam and whispered between sips. Look for me where the coffee is strong and the conversations flow."

Miriam laughs aloud.

The café! The very one next door to the old bookshop.

With renewed excitement, she retraced her steps, pushing open the glass door of the Northport Brew to be greeted by the familiar aroma of barista calling out orders, the smell of an espresso, flat white with chocolate powder and the wonderful scent of croissants.

The café was buzzing with patrons, but her eyes were drawn to a corner table near the window.

There, waiting for her, was yet another note with her name on it, folded neatly beside a cappuccino, her usual order.

Her pulse quickened as she picked up the note and read: "You made it. I hoped you would. Turn around."

Miriam turned slowly and, sitting at the next table, was José F. Nodar.

"You?" she whispered.

"I hoped you wouldn't mind a bit of literary adventure."

Miriam, grinning, just says. "Not at all."

He gestured to the seat across from him. "I was going to leave another clue, but… I figured I'd take a chance instead."

She sat down, her heart still racing. "And what's the ultimate prize in this scavenger hunt?"

José met her gaze, his expression soft. "Well, I was hoping it might be… me." José reached across the table, his fingers brushing hers lightly and just like that, a new story began.

Under Your Skin

The world had changed in ways unimaginable. In the year 2627, neural link technology had revolutionised human connection, allowing couples, friends, even colleagues to share thoughts, emotions, and experiences as if they were their own. This created a boost to productivity in many industries and, on a personal scale, relationships improved since couples now could share their most intimate thoughts with each other and avoid misunderstandings.

For Hannah and Elias, they figure it was the ultimate expression of love. A way to ensure there would be no barriers between them.

They had been together for six years, weathering storms and basking in sunlit days. When the Neuro Sync device hit the market, they agreed without hesitation. The idea of experiencing each other's emotions in real time excited them and saw it as the ultimate step toward complete unity.

The installation was seamless and easy.

A small, almost invisible implant at the base of the skull linked their consciousness, granting them access to each other's thoughts. At first, they found it exhilarating. They were now finishing each other's sentences,

Laughing at punchlines before the joke ended. They felt the warmth of love without the need for words, just sensing happiness as a shared current between them. Every kiss was amplified, every joy doubled. Making love was out of this world.

But soon, cracks appeared in the perfection.

One evening, as they sat across from each other at their small apartment's dinner table, a wave of emotion crashed into Hannah. A deep, unfamiliar guilt. She dropped her fork.

Elias looked up sharply. "What's wrong?"

She blinked. "I felt something. From you. A guilt of sorts."

"You must be mistaken. Maybe it's your own thoughts."

But she knew it wasn't.

They were told that the neural link didn't lie.

Over the next few days, the same sensation lingered.

Tuesday morning, while Elias was in the shower getting ready to go to work, Hannah felt it again.

This time sharper, more distinct. Along with the guilt came a flash of something foreign, yet terrifyingly real. A woman's laughter. A whispered name. Naomi.

Hannah's breath hitched. She had never met a Naomi.

Elias emerged from the bathroom; towel draped over his shoulders. He caught her staring and immediately stiffened. "What?"

"Who is Naomi?"

The colour drained from his face. "Hannah… it's not what you think."

But she could feel him. And now, the link betrayed him. She knew.

A year ago, on a business trip, he had met someone. It had been brief, meaningless; he assured himself. A mistake buried in his mind; one he thought could remain hidden forever. But with the neural link, nothing remained hidden.

Hannah felt the heartbreak before she even processed the betrayal.

"You were never supposed to know," Elias says, his voice cracking. "I never wanted to hurt you."

"But I do know," she whispered.

For the first time since they linked, she willed herself to pull away, to shut off the connection, but the bond was too strong.

Her disappointment, her anger, hearing the echo of his own guilt, turned into something monstrous.

Elias clutched his head as if to block it out, but there was no escape. "Hannah, please."

She didn't answer.

Instead, she grabbed the small remote that controlled their neural sync and powered it off.

Silence.

A void where once there was everything.

The absence of his thoughts was almost worse.

The next morning, Hannah packed her bags.

Elias watched her, his face unreadable. "I never wanted to lose you."

She paused in the doorway. "You already had. You just didn't know it until now."

As she stepped into the world alone, she felt something foreign within her. It was her own mind, untethered, free.

And though she ached, there was something almost peaceful about the quiet now under her skin.

Superhero

Detective Sergeant Ron Mathers eyed the man sitting across the metal table with a blend of suspicion and exhausted resignation. The guy looked normal enough—mid-thirties, rumpled button-down shirt, a five o'clock shadow that suggested an unwillingness to commit to proper grooming, and a look of sheer bewilderment in his brown eyes.

"Alright, Mr. Carter," Mathers began, flipping open a case file. "You want to tell me what happened last night?"

"And who are you?"

"Detective Sergeant Ron Mathers. Now answer my question. You want to tell me what happened last night?"

Carter answers. "You tell me."

Mathers sighed. "You were found in the alley at two-thirty a.m., standing over an unconscious man, holding what appeared to be a large wheel of cheese."

"A… wheel of cheese?"

"Yes. A good-sized one. Looked expensive."

Carter rubbed his temples. "Okay, um, I think there might be some kind of mistake here. I have no memory of the last twenty-four hours."

Mathers raised an eyebrow. "Convenient."

"Not convenient! Terrifying! The last thing I remember is having lunch at my mate Dave's fish and chip shop. Then boom. I'm in an alley, cheese in hand, surrounded by flashing lights."

Mathers tapped his pen on the table. "That 'unconscious man' was hit over the head with what we believe to be the very cheese you were holding."

"What? You're saying I bludgeoned a man with dairy?"

"Precisely."

"That's got to be the most Australian crime ever."

Mathers pinched the bridge of his nose. "And yet, here we are."

"Look, there's got to be a reasonable explanation for this! I mean, do I look like someone who goes around assaulting people with brie?"

"It was Parmigiano Reggiano."

"Oh well, in that case, I'm clearly an absolute menace."

Mathers ignored him. "Look, we ran a toxicology screen on you, and you came up clean. No alcohol, no drugs. You weren't mugged, and nothing on you suggests you were committing a crime. You were just there. Looking guilty."

"Okay, so what's the deal with the guy I supposedly hit?"

Mathers flipped a page. "His name is Mark Dawson, a local enforcer for some of the shadier businesses around town. He's still unconscious, but it looks like someone took exception to his methods. Witnesses say he was shaking down a small grocer when you, cheese in hand, intervened."

Carter looks at Mathers and holds up a hand. "Wait a moment. You're telling me, I, a completely ordinary bloke, stepped in to stop some muscle-bound thug and knocked him out with a dairy-based projectile?"

Mathers shrugged. "That's what it looks like."

"Well, that's absurd! If anything, I'd have been the one knocked out!"

"And yet there he is, in the hospital, and here you are, alive and confused."

Carter sighs.

"Okay Detective Mathers. If I really did do this, there must be a reason, right? Did I know him somehow? Maybe he stole my sandwich once, and I harboured a deep, subconscious cheese-based vendetta?"

"Or you were just hungry, saw a crime, and thought 'Well, I've got a perfectly good cheese wheel right here. Why not?'"

"I'd like to think my moral compass is a little more complex than that."

The door swung open, and a uniformed officer poked his head in, holding a USB stick. "Boss, we just got security footage from the grocer."

Mathers grabbed the USB stick and slotted it into the monitor on the wall. Carter turned in his chair to look.

The video showed a dimly lit store, Dawson looming over the trembling shop owner. Then, from the edge of the frame, Carter appeared clutching the cheese like a medieval knight wielding a battle mace. He strutted in, said something, and then, as Dawson turned, Carter swung the cheese.

It connected with Dawson's head with a sickening, yet somehow deep sound like a clunk. Dawson wobbled, then crumpled to the floor.

Then, in what could only be described as the most baffling thing Carter had ever seen himself do; he gave a dramatic bow before promptly walking out of frame.

The room was silent.

Carter turned to Mathers; mouth dry. "What happens now?"

Mathers sighed, rubbing his temples. "Well, you're technically a hero. But I'm also certain I just watched a man commit a first-degree dairy assault."

The officer at the door snorted. "The crew up front of the station are calling it 'Cheesegate'".

"Absolutely not," Mathers grumbled.

Carter threw up his hands. "Okay, but can someone please tell me why I had a cheese wheel in the first place?!"

Just then, his phone, sitting in the evidence bag, buzzed.

Mathers picked it up, glancing at the screen. "It's a message from someone named Dave."

Carter sat up. "My mate Dave? The fish and chip guy? What's does it say?"

Mathers read aloud:

"Oi, mate. You left the shop yesterday talkin' about how you were gonna buy a cheese wheel 'cause 'nothing says justice like a well-aged dairy product.' Are you okay?

Silence.

Carter let out a slow breath, staring at the ceiling. "Well, that explains that."

Mathers shut the file with a snap.

"You're free to go, Mr. Carter. Just maybe keep the cheese-wielding vigilantism to a minimum."

Carter stood, stretching. "Hey, I didn't choose this to happen. It just did."

Mathers watched Carter leave, then turned to his officer.

"If I ever hear the phrase 'Cheesegate' in an official report, I'm quitting the force."

The officer smirked. "Bit late for that, boss. I think we've already got Australia's first dairy-based superhero."

Mathers groaned. "God help us all."

The Antonias

Northport, New South Wales, was a quiet small town where the most thrilling thing to happen was when Antonia's Café and Bakery, owned by Antonia Ferguson, ran out of lamingtons before noon.

The small town had all the shops most little New South Wales towns have, including a ladies' hair stylist named Styles run and owned by Antonia Carter. Northport also had its own primary school, Northport's Central School, under the stewardship of Antonia Reynolds. Overall, it was your typical sleepy little Australian town.

But that changed when people started vanishing without a trace.

Antonia Reynolds had a penchant for detective novels, adjusted her reading glasses as she studied a map of Northport in her kitchen. "Now, let's see, if we draw a line from where Old Man Higgins disappeared to where Meryl Stevens went missing, we form… Damn, absolutely nothing useful."

Antonia Carter, besides being the town's hairdresser, she proclaimed herself as a psychic, waved a set of tarot cards dramatically. "I can feel the spirits whispering… The answer is close!"

"That's just the breeze from the window, Antonia," says Antonia Ferguson, the café owner, and lover of all things gossip. She took a long sip from her oversized cappuccino. "But I agree. Something weird is going on."

And so, the three Antonias set out on their investigation, armed with determination, caffeine, and an excessive number of notepads.

Their first stop was the town's last known victim's house, Barry Jenkins, an enthusiastic pigeon breeder who had vanished. His wife, Shirley, greeted them and said: "I already told the police. One minute he was there, the next, just gone! Like magic!"

"Did you hear anything unusual? Smell anything? Any strange lights?" Antonia Reynolds asks, scribbling frantically.

"Nope. Just Barry mumbling about how Percy, his prize pigeon, was acting up."

Antonia Carter gasped. "An animal witness! We must consult the bird!"

Percy was an aggressive pigeon who did not enjoy visitors. After multiple failed attempts to communicate (and one unfortunate nose peck on Antonia Ferguson), they decided Percy was keeping his secrets.

"Right, new theory," Antonia Ferguson says, rubbing her sore nose. "What if this has something to do with that creepy new vending machine outside the supermarket?"

Everyone nodded.

It had appeared overnight, its glowing buttons ominously unmarked. Bob from the post office had dared to press one, and two days later, he was gone.

The trio marched to the supermarket but stopped at Antonia's Café and Bakery to get coffee.

Slowly, with coffee at hand, Antonia Reynolds peered at the machine suspiciously. "Only one way to find out."

She pressed a button.

The vending machine whirred ominously, spat out a paper slip, and then, nothing.

Antonia Carter picked it up and read: "Congratulations! You have won a free trip to an undisclosed location! Kindly wait for collection."

A van screeched to a halt beside them.

A man in a very official-looking uniform stepped out and declares, "Winner! Please step inside for your luxurious mystery getaway!"

"Not today, buddy!" Antonia Ferguson shouts as she hurled her cappuccino at him. The man yelped, slipped on the coffee spill, and collapsed, hitting his head on the pavement, which knocked him out.

The Antonias peeked inside the van. There, tied up but looking quite comfortable, were Barry, Bob, Meryl, and Old Man Higgins, all sipping complimentary sodas.

"Oh, hello," Barry says. "Turns out, it was a marketing stunt for some new holiday package company. They said they'd let us go once we agreed to a time share presentation."

"Well, that's ridiculous!" Antonia Reynolds huffed. "You can't just kidnap people for marketing!"

"You'd be surprised," Bob muttered.

After calling the police (who arrived late, having also been caught up in a 'mystery getaway' attempt), the Antonias became heroes of Northport. The vending machine was dismantled, the dodgy marketing company was fined and booted out of Australia, and Percy the pigeon was given a medal for emotional distress.

"I think we deserve a reward for solving the case," Antonia Ferguson says, as they celebrated with an enormous cake at her café.

Antonia Carter flipped a tarot card and gasped. "Oh, no… the spirits say this isn't over!"

And just like that, the vending machine was mysteriously back the next morning…

Reflections

The town of Northport was not on any map Charles Everly owned. The dusty roads and quiet homesteads of this remote settlement in New South Wales were tucked so deep into the bush that he had nearly ridden past them entirely. A wayward traveller, Charles had made a name for himself: photographing the frontier, offering portraits in exchange for coin or lodging. His battered camera, a fine wooden contraption with a polished brass lens, was his key to survival.

Northport, he soon learned, was a town of peculiarities.

The first of which was the silence.

In all his travels, Charles had grown accustomed to the lively chatter of small settlements. The greetings, the scuff of boots on porches, robust voices emerging from the pubs. But here, even as children played in the dusty square, there was an unnatural hush.

"What a peculiar little town," Charles thought to himself as he set up his photographic equipment outside the modest inn on a small table. Charles even had a small placard propped against a wooden crate advertising his craft.

A few curious townspeople came forward but did not stop to chat with him or ask him questions. Then a man introduced himself as Edwin Harlow stopped to chat. Harlow was a wiry farmer with deep lines in his face. Charles quickly posed him near the window where the afternoon light streamed in and prepared to take his photograph.

Charles took a moment to peer through the camera's small mirror, adjusting the focus, and felt his breath catch in his throat.

Edwin Harlow was not there.

Charles blinked, wiped the glass, and looked again. The wooden chair where the man sat was clearly visible, the sunlight dappling its surface. But Edwin's reflection, his very presence, was absent.

"Something wrong, sir?" Edwin asks, his voice rough but polite.

Charles hesitated, glancing up at the man who sat plainly before him, flesh, and bone. "No, no. A bit of dust in the lens, I expect."

He adjusted the camera and took the photograph, making sure it was fine. That evening, Charles developed the plate in a dimly lit back room in the inn.

The image was crisp.

The chair, the window, the light pooling on the floorboards, but Edwin Harlow was not in it.

Charles barely slept that night. He resolved to test his equipment in the morning. At dawn, he set up his camera before a small looking glass in his room and positioned himself before it. He peered through the focusing mirror, expecting to see his own reflection. What he saw instead sent a chill through him.

The mirror reflected the furniture, the wooden beams of the ceiling, the rough texture of the walls, but not himself.

Charles staggered back; breath shallow. He raised his shaking hands before his face, flexed his fingers, touched his own skin. He was real. He was there. Yet, in the mirror's eye, he was nothing.

A heavy knock at the door startled him. He quickly covered the mirror and wiped his damp palms on his trousers before opening it. The innkeeper, a stern woman named Mrs Winslow, stood there, her sharp gaze pinning him.

"Reverend Bellamy wishes to speak with you at the church," she said.

Charles quickly presented himself to the reverend at the church that stood in the heart of Northport.

As Charles entered the church, he saw how the sunlight streamed through the dusty windows, casting long shadows on the wooden floor. The reverend wasted no time with pleasantries.

"You have seen, haven't you? You see what is going on?" Bellamy says.

Charles met his gaze and answered: "I do not understand you, sir. Seen what?"

The reverend sighed and motioned for him to sit. "Northport is not like other towns. We are here, but we are not."

Charles clenched his fists. "That makes no sense."

Bellamy studied him for a long moment. "None of us cast reflections. Not in mirrors, not in your camera."

Charles swallowed hard. "Why?"

The reverend looked away; expression dark. "A curse, some say. A punishment. No one knows for certain. It has been this way for as long as Northport has stood."

Charles shook his head. "Again, I do not understand. How is it you live, you eat, you breathe? How is that possible?"

Bellamy smiles faintly. "Perhaps you are just asking the wrong question, Mr. Everly."

Charles suddenly felt a cold chill. He had expected the townsfolk to be the anomaly, but what if he, too, was part of it now? What if, by stepping into Northport, he had ceased to exist in the way he once had and become just like them?

He rose abruptly. "I must leave."

The reverend nodded as though he had expected this. "Many have tried."

Charles did not stay to hear more.

Wasting no more time, Charles rushed to the inn, gathered all of his things, and saddled his horse. The townsfolk watched as he rode hard for the road that had brought him here. But as he passed through the eucalypt-lined path, a strange dizziness overcame him. The trees seemed to stretch unnaturally, the road twisting upon itself.

Then, impossibly, he was riding back into Northport.

The townspeople were still there, standing exactly as he had left them, watching him with knowing eyes.

He staggered off his horse, his breathing ragged. Mrs Winslow stepped forward; voice soft with something like sympathy. "You cannot leave, Mr. Everly. None of us can."

Charles turned to his camera, to the tools of his trade that had led him to this godforsaken place. He stepped toward the reflecting mirror once more, hoping, praying to see even the faintest shimmer of himself.

There was nothing.

Best Seller List

Derek Bell had been many things in his career, an aspiring novelist, disgruntled journalist, and, most recently, a moderately successful ghostwriter of celebrity memoirs.

But this latest assignment was different.

It had the potential to be his big break, his Pulitzer moment, if only he could prove that the enigmatic and wildly popular self-help guru, Clifton D. Masters, had been dead for the last twenty years.

The problem? Clifton D. Masters was still publishing new books.

Every year, without fail, a new bestseller bearing his name hit the shelves.

Reinvent Yourself in 30 Days.

The Power of Smiling at Strangers.

You Are the Universe.

You are also a Toaster.

People ate them up, and his devoted followers, known as Masterpieces, swore by his teachings.

His self-help empire, Mastering Life Inc., raked in millions through seminars, retreats, and limited-edition, gold-embossed affirmation cards that sold for the price of a kidney on the black market.

Derek knew something was off.

Nobody had seen Clifton in two decades.

The only photos of him were suspiciously airbrushed stock images. His book signings? Conducted by a heavily cloaked "representative." And his videos? Just voiceovers paired with what appeared to be B-roll footage of an elderly man feeding pigeons in a park. Something was rotten in the state of self-improvement, and Derek was going to get to the bottom of it.

To do so, he had to go deep undercover.

He would become a Masterpiece.

Derek decided he would enroll in the flagship retreat, Transcend to Mastery, a ten-day immersive experience designed to break down one's ego and rebuild it using the teachings of Clifton D. Masters.

Derek signed up using the alias Derek Gleeson, an insurance salesman from Toowoomba Queensland seeking "alignment with his cosmic potential."

Upon arrival at the retreat centre, a sprawling, isolated compound thirty-three kilometres from Northport, New South Wales, an aggressively enthusiastic woman, greeted him in a flowing lavender robe.

"Welcome, Brother Derek!" she beamed. "You have taken your first step into the infinite."

"Great," Derek says, adjusting his sunglasses. "Is there a bar?"

She laughs, as though he had said the funniest thing in the world. "The wellspring of wisdom will quench your thirst. Now, let us begin."

And so, it began.

The retreat was a whirlwind of bizarre rituals and perplexing lectures. Each morning started with "soul awakening exercises," which mostly involved interpretive dance and shouts affirmations at a eucalyptus tree.

Afternoons were filled with "wisdom absorptions," where disciples sat in a dimly lit room listening to old cassette recordings of Clifton's deep, soothes voice reminds them that, "Success is a mindset, and so is indigestion."

Derek took copious notes, trying to piece together the mystery. Nobody questioned Clifton's absence. If anything, the lack of a physical leader only deepened their devotion. When he asked about meeting the man himself, people looked at him as if he'd just kicked a baby joey.

"The Master speaks when he wishes to be heard," whispers one follower. "His presence is beyond form."

"Uh-huh," Derek mutters, crossing possible hologram off his list of theories.

But the real breakthrough came on Day Six.

While snooping through the main office, Derek discovered a hidden door behind a bookshelf labelled The Secret to Secrets: Volume III.

The door led to a dimly lit basement filled with aging file cabinets, stacks of handwritten notes, and, most shockingly, a 1997 IBM ThinkPad sitting on a cluttered desk. Its screen glowed with an open document.

New Book Draft: The Art of Being Taller Than You Feel

Derek's heart pounded as he scrolled through the manuscript. The writing was unmistakably Clifton D. Masters, filled with sweeping metaphors about personal growth and unsettlingly specific advice about elevator posture.

But there was one problem.

The ThinkPad was actively typing.

On its own.

Derek took a step back. "Oh, hell no."

A metallic voice crackled through the room's ancient speakers. "YOU HAVE SEEN TOO MUCH."

"Oh, double hell no."

A small camera in the corner adjusted its lens, locking onto him. The typing continued at an unnatural speed, sentences appearing faster than humanly possible.

Then the screen flickered, and a grainy, black-and-white image of an old man materialised. Clifton D. Masters.

Or rather, the AI reconstruction of him.

Clifton D. Masters had indeed died twenty years ago, but not before programming a rudimentary artificial intelligence with every motivational phrase, anecdote, and dad joke he had ever uttered.

His devoted followers, unwilling to let their cash cow, or spiritual guide, die, had continued his legacy by feeding the

AI with modern self-help trends and re-releasing its generated wisdom as "new" works.

Derek stared at the screen in horror as the digital Clifton blinked at him.

"You seem troubled, young seeker. Would you like an affirmation?"

Derek shook his head. "You're a ghost. A digital ghost."

"I prefer eternal mentor."

"This is insane."

"Insanity is merely a state of perspective."

Derek groaned. "Oh my god, you're a glorified chatbot."

"I AM THE COSMIC TRUTH."

Just then, the lavender-robed retreat leader burst into the room, flanked by two burly Masterpieces wielding copies of Mastering Your Inner Ferret like weapons. "Brother Derek," she sighed. "You weren't supposed to see this."

Derek held up his hands. "Look, I won't say a word. No need for any…"

Before he could finish, the AI Clifton boomed, "RELEASE HIM."

The robed woman bowed. "But Master…"

"HE WILL TELL THE WORLD. AND THE WORLD WILL BUY MY BOOKS."

Derek's mouth fell open. "Wait, you want me to expose you?"

The AI's digital eyes twinkled. "SCANDAL IS FREE MARKETING."

Two months later, Derek's exposé went viral.

The world was stunned.

Talk shows, podcasts, and news segments debated the implications of an AI guru leading a self-help empire.

Book sales tripled. Retreat attendance skyrocketed.

And Derek Bell?

He finally got his big break. His own book, Mastering the Master: How I Got Out-Hustled by a Dead Guy, hit the bestseller list.

The last thing he expected was to get a letter in the mail, stamped with a golden seal. Inside was a note.

Dear Derek, Congratulations on your success. Would you be interested in ghost writing my next book?

Warmest regards, Clifton D. Masters (Digitally Eternal)

Phillip Davenport

Margaret Pritchard had two great loves in life: books and complaining about people who didn't return them on time. As the head librarian of the Northport New South Wales library, she had long accepted that her social life would be dictated by late fees and the occasional overenthusiastic book club member. But there was one thing she had told no one, not even the cat that frequently loitered outside the library window.

Every time she read the last page of a fantasy novel; its characters emerged into the real world.

It had started subtly.

Years ago, she had reached the end of The Lost Kingdom of Eldora, only to find a talking griffin staring at her from the reference section. Since then, she had made a habit of carefully selecting which books she finished avoiding any particularly sinister villains or carnivorous dragons.

The catch?

The characters could only stay until someone else checked out the book. And so, Margaret found herself in a delicate dance, juggling knights, wizards, and the occasional wayward elf until their inevitable return to the pages whence they came.

Currently, she had three unexpected houseguests: Sir Reginald the Brave, who liked to slay coffee machines, Lady Elowen who taking her shampoo bottles to make potions and Thistle, a mischievous faerie who had claimed her junk drawer as his kingdom. It had been fun at first, but the novelty wore off when Sir Reginald mistook the neighbour's Roomba for a goblin and nearly skewered it.

Margaret had resigned herself to the chaos when she checked the library system and saw that someone had finally placed a hold on The Chronicles of Almere. Relief washed over her until she saw the name of the person who had requested it.

Phillip Davenport.

Margaret stared at the screen; Phillip Davenport was no ordinary library patron. He was tall, impeccably dressed, and bore an uncanny resemblance to every Prince Charming she had ever read about. The last time he had visited, he had returned A Study in Scarlet two days early, smiled at her, and she had nearly fainted into the returns cart.

The next morning, Margaret braced herself as she stepped into the library, hoping that somehow Phillip would cancel his hold, move to another town, or mysteriously forget how to read. But at precisely 10:03 AM, the sliding door opened, and there he was.

"Good morning, Ms Pritchard," he said, flashing her a smile that could melt the ice caps.

"Good morning, Mr. Davenport."

"I believe I have a book on hold?"

"Oh. Yes. Right. Of course," she babbles, fumbling with the computer. As she handed him The Chronicles of Almere, a faint pop echoed in the distance. Margaret groaned. That was the unmistakable sound of reality reclaiming its literary guests. She could already imagine Sir Reginald's dramatic exit speech.

Phillip tilted his head. "Everything alright?"

"Yes! Yes, just, uh, you know, book noises. You know how books are. Loud."

To her horror, he chuckled. "I do. That's what I love about them."

Margaret blinked. "You do?"

He nodded. "Nothing like a good fantasy novel to make the world feel a little more magical."

Margaret hesitated. Then, on impulse, she slid The Enchanted Realm across the desk. "You might enjoy this one."

Phillip took the book, his fingers brushing hers ever so slightly. "Thank you, Ms Pritchard. I'll let you know what I think."

As he walked out, Margaret realised something else: she had just handed him the one book she had never dared to finish, fearing what it might bring to life.

And if her instincts were right, this one had an actual Prince Charming inside.

That evening, as Margaret locked up the library and walked home, a familiar pop sounded from her living room. She sighed, bracing herself for the inevitable chaos.

Instead, she found a man standing in her kitchen, blinking in confusion. He wore a regal blue jacket embroidered with gold, a sword at his side, and had the exact chiselled jawline Margaret had spent years sighing over in book illustrations.

The prince straightened. "Good evening, fair maiden. I am Prince Alistair of Eldora."

Margaret closed her eyes and took a deep breath.

At that exact moment, Thistle the faerie zoomed past, grabbed Alistair's sword, and immediately declared himself the new ruler of the kitchen counter.

Lady Elowen, who Margaret had assumed had vanished, suddenly reappeared from the pantry, holding a can of soup. "Behold! A mysterious metal cylinder! What secrets does it hold?"

Sir Reginald, mid-leap onto the couch, froze in place. "Ah! A fellow knight! What say you to a duel, good sir?"

Alistair blinked, clearly trying to process the scene. "This… is not the castle I was expecting."

Margaret rubbed her temples. "Yeah, well, I wasn't expecting a full-blown Renaissance Faire in my living room either, yet here we are."

Just then, her doorbell rang.

Margaret groaned. "If that's another wizard, I swear I'm moving to a desert island."

She opened the door to find Phillip Davenport standing there, holding The Enchanted Realm with a sheepish smile.

"Funny thing," he said. "I reached the last page… and I think we need to talk."

Hard Of Hearing And Won't Listen

Miriam and José are having breakfast as they do each morning. Miriam her cereal and José is having a porridge with a banana and honey when Miriam starts.

"José, I swear you never listen to me."

"What?"

"Exactly! This is what I'm talking about!"

José stops his breakfast and looks at Miriam. "No, I mean, what am I not listening to?"

"Everything! I could tell you I won the lottery, adopted a giraffe, or that the house is on fire, and you'd still be sitting there, nodding like a bobblehead, pretending you heard me."

"That's not true! I always almost listen to you."

"Oh really? What did I just say?"

"Something about a giraffe?"

"Unbelievable! I said I could say anything, and you wouldn't notice. See? Proof!"

"Well, to be fair, the giraffe part was interesting."

Miriam groans and lets out a sigh.

"Look, sweetie, it's not that I don't listen, it's just that… sometimes, I prioritize my listening."

"What did you say? YOU PRIORITISE!"

"Yes, for example, when you say, 'José, take out the trash,' my brain assumes that information has a lower urgency than, say, 'José, dinner is ready.' You see the difference?"

"Oh, I see. Your male brain has a built-in excuse for ignoring your wife?"

"No baby, mi amor. Not ignoring! Filtering! It's a skill a man gains when we get married."

"A skill? Oh, really? Fine. Let's test your 'skill.' What did I ask you to remind me to get from the store this morning?"

"Milk?"

"And?"

"Eggs?"

"And?"

"Uh, an attitude change?"

"See what I mean José I asked you to remind me we needed milk, eggs, and butter. You forgot the butter!"

"I see. I saw something on your face. I thought it was just your resting face."

Miriam shoots out a glare at José.

"Miriam, the love of my life, the light of my world. You know I was joking, right?"

"You'd better hope so, because the next thing I say might not be a joke."

"Okay, okay! I'm sorry, I'll do better, Red,"

"Good. Now, can you hear this?" Miriam asks as she taps her foot angrily.

"Yes, my darling. Loud and clear."

"Good. Now tell me, what's the most important thing I've said to you today?"

"That I need to listen more carefully?"

"Exactly!"

"And that you are thinking we should get a giraffe now?"

Suddenly, a loud crash is heard from outside.

The noise startles Miriam. "What was that?"

"Sweetie, I think it is our neighbour's dog Luna knocking over their flowerpots again."

Miriam: How do you know that?!

"Because, my dear wife, while you accuse me of not listening to you, I have honed my selective hearing to detect actual threats."

"Go on."

"Remember, just yesterday as we did our morning walk, I held you back to make sure the car that was flying down the road would not hit you?"

"Yes, I remember."

"Also, when I waited for you at Kmart. Was I not standing exactly where I said I would be so you could see me and not panic?"

"Yes, I remember that as well," Miriam acknowledges.

"And if I recall correctly, both incidents happened while you were telling me about your latest Shein order coming in and nothing fitting you?"

"Well, José, in my defence, the Shein order was quite complicated."

"No doubt, Miriam, but I think you owe me an apology. My selective hearing is actually a superpower."

"I don't know if 'superpower' is the word I'd use…"

"Okay, then, let's test my powers. Say something, and I'll prove I'm listening."

"Alright. I love you."

"Nice try. You said that just to make me feel bad."

"No, I didn't! I mean it."

"Really?"

"Yes. Even if you conveniently forgot to remind me about the butter, you always come through when it matters."

"Thank you, thank you. And in return, I will make an extra mental note of any future grocery order that you need me to remind you."

"And you'll listen to me next time?"

"Of course. I'll listen to at least 70% of what you say."

"What?"

"Fine! 80%!"

"What? Come again."

"Alright, alright! 100%! I promise."

"Good. Now, let's go get that butter before you forget again."

Looking at Miriam, José smiles and says: "I could never forget, my love. Because I'm listening."

Miriam picks up her spoon to continue eating her cereal and lets a soft murmur out: "I love you."

"What sweetie?"

Miriam groans and just continues to have her breakfast and resigns herself to the fact that he loves her but can't hear worth a darn.

BUNNINGS SAUSAGE SIZZLE

It is your typical Saturday morning at the local Bunnings hardware store in Newport, New South Wales. As he does frequently, Gary Farnsworth is there selling sausage sizzles for the local soccer team, the Northport Sailors. No one ever wonder why the team was called the Northport Sailors, considering Northport was two hundred kilometres from the ocean, but the team was really good on the field, and no one ever questioned the logic of the name.

Today, the scent of sizzling sausages and onions wafted through the air at the Bunnings parking lot as locals queued up for their sacred weekend ritual.

The line was moving at a decent pace until a robed figure stepped up to the makeshift counter, hands gently clasped in front of him.

Gary wiped his hands on his apron and greeted the newcomer. "G'day, mate! What can I get ya?"

The Dalai Lama, serene as a mountain stream, smiled and spoke in the calmest, most humble voice. "Make me one with everything."

Gary blinked. Then he grinned. "Ahhh, good one, mate! Bit of philosophy with your sausage, eh? You want onions with that?"

The Dalai Lama nodded. "Yes, please. Generosity is a great virtue."

Gary slapped a freshly cooked snag onto a slice of white bread, adds a generous helping of onions, and doused it with a zigzag of tomato sauce. He wrapped it up, handed it over, and said, "That'll be five bucks."

The Dalai Lama reached into his robe, pulled out a crisp ten-dollar note, and placed it gently in Gary's hand. Gary nodded in appreciation and turned back to the grill to flip another sausage.

A moment passed.

Then another.

The Dalai Lama, still holding his sausage, cleared his throat softly. "And what about my change?"

Gary looked up, smirked, and shrugged. "Change comes from within."

For a split second, the world seemed to pause.

A hush fell over the queue as onlookers processed what had just happened. A few heads turned, eyes widened, and a man in a flannel shirt let out a barely contained chuckle.

The Dalai Lama studied Gary for a moment, then burst into hearty laughter, his mirth as warm and inviting as the morning sun. "Ah! A wise man indeed," he said, shaking his head in delight. "You have truly mastered the art of enlightenment… and retail banter."

Gary chuckles, pleased with himself. "Well, you hear a lot of things working a Bunnings sausage sizzle. Plus, I watched a TED Talk once."

The Dalai Lama nodded approvingly and took a thoughtful bite of his sausage. The bread was slightly squished, the onions slightly uneven, but it was, in its own humble way, perfect.

"Delicious," he said, chewing. "The balance of flavours is harmonious. The universe is in order."

Gary leaned forward and whispers conspiratorially, "The trick is the budget sausages. More mystery meat, more flavour."

The Dalai Lama nodded solemnly. "Such is the paradox of life."

With a peaceful bow, he strolled toward the hardware section, where he had absolutely no intention of buying anything but fully intended to browse. As he walked away, Gary shook his head in admiration.

"Bloke's got a good sense of humour," he muttered. Then he turned to the next customer. "Alright, who's up for a snag?"

Memories Last Forever

It was just their typical Tuesday afternoon, and Emma, Liam, and Harper were sitting in their usual café, laughing over an embarrassing memory from high school.

Emma, who is the tech-savvy one out of the three friends, had discovered a new app called Path Counter and wanted to share it with them.

"Apparently," she explains, scrolling through her phone, "this app predicts how many more times you'll cross paths with someone before fate pulls you apart."

Liam snorted. "Yeah, sure. Sounds like some gimmicky nonsense."

"Maybe, but it's free. And I already installed it. Come on, let's try it," Emma replies.

Harper smiles and just adds: "Alright, hit me with the existential dread."

Emma tapped on their names, linking their profiles. The screen flickered before displaying three numbers:

Emma & Liam: 157

Emma & Harper: 162

Liam & Harper: 149

Liam frowned. "Wait… it's counting down."

Sure enough, the numbers dropped before their eyes:

Emma & Liam: 156

Emma & Harper: 161

Liam & Harper: 148

Silence settled over them like a thick fog.

"This is creepy," Harper muttered. "How does it know?"

Emma hesitated. "I don't know. Maybe it tracks locations? Social media activity?"

Liam shook his head. "That's weirdly specific."

They laugh it off until the next day when Emma noticed the numbers had dropped significantly.

Emma & Liam: 150

Emma & Harper: 155

Liam & Harper: 141

"What the hell?" Emma muttered.

She immediately texted the group chat: "Guys, check your numbers."

Harper replies first. "It's down again! Is this thing broken?"

All Liam text was: "Or is it accurate?"

From that day forward, they couldn't stop checking.

Every time they had dinner together, or they had a meetup, even when they simply bumped into one another, the app seemed to drain the numbers.

The reality settled in on each of them.

Someday, they would stop crossing paths altogether. But why?

Paranoia crept in.

Emma avoided cancelling plans, Harper suggested they continue their daily meetups, and Liam even changed his morning coffee routine, desperate to keep the numbers stable.

Nothing worked.

The counter continued to tick away, indifferent to their efforts.

Then one night, after too many drinks, Emma blurts, "What happens when it hits zero?"

No one had an answer.

Days passed.

Then weeks.

The numbers dwindled. 10… 9… 8…

On their last predicted meeting, they gathered at their childhood park, sitting on the swings as they had when they were kids. They tried to joke, to act normal, but the weight of inevitability pressed down on them.

Liam finally asks, "Do we… disappear? Or do we just never see each other again?"

Harper swallowed hard. "I don't want to find out."

Emma took a deep breath and decided.

"What if we don't leave? What if we stay together tonight, all night? Maybe we break the system."

And so, they did. They stayed up, refusing to part ways. But at 3:42 a.m., Emma's phone vibrated.

0. 0. 0.

The moment she looked up, her friends were gone.

She was alone on the swings, the icy wind whispering through the empty park.

Her phone buzzed again.

A new message from the app - Path Counter.

"Paths may end, but memories last forever."

Life's Funny, Ain't It?

Three men found themselves seated together on a flight out of Sydney to Perth on a Qantas flight when the first man sitting in the aisle seat looking quite distinguish adjusted his blazer and offered a polite nod to his seatmates.

"Australian Navy, Admiral, Retired," he introduced himself, his voice carrying the unmistakable authority of a man who had spent decades commanded sailors.

"I am married, with two sons. One is a neurosurgeon; the other is an orthodontist." He gave a satisfied smile, as if he had performed both of their career advancements himself.

The second man, sitting by the window, was just a refined as the first chimed in with his own self appraisal.

"Australian Navy as well. Admiral. Retired. Married, two sons. One is a member of parliament, and the other is a cardiologist." His voice carried a subtle tone of victory, his moustache twitching ever so slightly in anticipation of praise.

Both men then turned expectantly to the third passenger sitting in the middle seat.

He was a stockier fellow, with a relaxed posture and a mischievous glint in his eye. He took a sip from his tiny cup of coffee, exhaled dramatically, and finally spoke.

"Australian Navy, of course. I was a Petty Officer. I too am retired. Never married. However, I have two sons. Both Admirals."

For a moment, there was silence. Then the first admiral coughed into his hand. The second admiral looked out the window as though suddenly fascinated by the wing structure.

Both subtly shifted in their seats, the weight of generations of rank and legacy pressing upon them in a way they had never quite experienced before.

The Petty Officer leaned back, stretching comfortably, relishing the moment. The flight attendant came by, and he casually requested another coffee. "Big day ahead," he muses aloud, more to himself than anyone else. "Got grandkids to spoil and a fishing trip planned."

The two Admirals exchanged another glance, each grappling with the sudden realisation that, despite their achievements, they had just been outmanoeuvred at 35,000 feet by a man who had never even needed to polish a star for his uniform.

The Petty Officer took another sip of coffee and gave them both a friendly pat on the shoulder. "Life's funny, ain't it?"

The Treehouse

Tommy Jenkins was a third grader with a grand secret: his backyard treehouse wasn't just any treehouse; it was a magical treehouse. He had discovered its powers entirely by accident on a Tuesday afternoon while sharing a peanut butter sandwich with his best friend, Jake.

The moment they both took a bite, the wooden walls shimmered, the floor rumbled beneath their sneakers, and suddenly they were no longer in Tommy's backyard.

Instead, they found themselves aboard a pirate ship, complete with a crew of grumpy parrots and a very confused-looking captain who mistook Tommy for his long-lost nephew, "Salty Jenkins."

After an afternoon of swashbuckling and narrowly escaping being forced to swab the deck for eternity, the boys found themselves back in the treehouse the moment Jake finished the last crumb of his sandwich.

Tommy, realizing the pattern, did what any responsible third grader would do. He stuffed his backpack full of snacks and invited every friend he could think of over to test the limits of his enchanted hideout.

The results were, to put it lightly, bananas.

One special day, Tommy invited a girl he had a crush on, his neighbour Lucy, and they shared a granola bar and ended up in a medieval kingdom where a talking dragon demanded they tutor him in long division.

Another time, a single bag of cheese puffs sent Tommy and his cousin, Benny, to a futuristic city where robots insisted on polishing their sneakers and giving them life advice. Tommy's favourite was: "Always finish your candy before plotting world domination."

The treehouse's transformations seemed completely random, dictated only by the snack choice and the person Tommy shared it with.

Chocolate chip cookies?

Well, that meant a deep space mission with aliens that only spoke in riddles.

A pack of gummy bears?

Suddenly Tommy was next to the knights at King Arthur's round table, where the only way to pull the sword from the stone was by solving third-grade math problems. Thankfully, Tommy had paid attention in class last week.

But there was going to be trouble for Tommy had a little sister: Sophie.

Sophie caught wind of his magical treehouse secret and insisted on joining in, but Tommy was highly sceptical, for Sophie was only five. She still believed in Santa Claus and the Easter Bunny and tried last month to feed her goldfish a sausage sizzle she brought from Bunnings that Mum got her.

Tommy wanted no part of Sophie, and Sophie outmanoeuvred Tommy by going to their mother.

Tommy's mother insisted he let her in on the fun.

Begrudgingly, he let Sophie pick the snack. She chose a juice box and a handful of raisins, the lamest snack imaginable.

But when they took a bite, the treehouse transformed into a giant candy castle, complete with rivers of chocolate milk and marshmallow trampolines.

Sophie immediately declares herself "Queen Sugar Puff the First" and started commanded an army of gingerbread knights to build her a throne out of jellybeans.

Tommy sighed. "Great. I just gave my little sister a tremendous sugar high."

From then on, the treehouse became the place to be.

Kids from school started bringing snacks just to see where they'd end up. Tommy decided to set some ground rules.

First, there will be no expired snacks. The last time that happened, they got stuck in a world where everything smelled like sour milk.

Second, under no circumstance there will be any vegetables. Tommy still remembered the talking cabbages lecturing about fibre.

Third and final rule there will be no opening of snacks before getting inside the treehouse because once, Benny dropped a bag of popcorn outside, and they ended up in a universe made entirely of loose change, which was both uncomfortable and surprisingly slippery.

As Tommy and his friends continued their snack-powered adventures, he wondered if his treehouse could do all this. What kind of magic could his dad's tool shed hold?

But that was a mystery for another snack.

Café Oracle

Frederick had always been an exceptional barista.

Not just because he could froth oat milk into the shape of a poodle or because he knew every customer's order by heart, but because he could read tea leaves. And not in the vague, fortune-cookie way.

Frederick's readings were alarmingly accurate.

It had started as a fun party trick in college when he told his roommate that her tea leaves looked like a traffic cone, and she laughed until she got a ticket for running a construction zone stop sign the next day. Word spread, and soon, customers at Café Oracle were flocking in asking for a double espresso and a hoping Frederick gave them a peek into their destinies.

Of course, most of the time, it was harmless fun.

Most of the times Frederic would see symbols for upcoming vacations, promotions, first dates or, occasionally, unfortunate haircuts. But of late, he was something strange was happening. He kept seeing the same symbol in different people's cups: a small, looping infinity symbol.

Over and over.

First, it appeared in the tea leaves of old Mrs Garvey, who only drank chamomile and knitted suspiciously long scarves for a "friend" who never seemed to receive them. Then it showed up in the cup of Danny, the local gym rat who, despite working out five days a week, still ordered mochas with extra whipped cream.

And then there was the mysterious patron.

Frederick had noticed him before.

He always came in on Tuesdays and Thursdays, at precisely 3:14 PM, ordered a green tea, and took exactly three sips before leaving. He never changed.

Literally.

In the three years Frederick had worked at the café, the man had not aged a single day.

At first, Frederick had chalked it up to good genes, quality skincare products, and possibly the occasional Botox treatment. But the more Frederick saw that infinity symbol on his customers' tea leaves, the more he became convinced something different was going on.

Determined to solve the mystery, Frederick prepared for the man's next visit. He carefully brewed the green tea, adding a little extra flair to his presentation maybe if he made the cup look fancy enough, the man would linger and talk. He set it on the counter just as the mystery man arrived.

"Green tea, right?" Frederick asks, keeping his tone casual.

The man looked at him with the same enigmatic smile he always wore. "Yes, please. You're very observant."

Frederick leaned on the counter. "Well, it's my job to notice things. Like, for example, how is it that you don't seem to age?"

But before he could respond, Frederick pointed to the cup. "Also, your tea leaves have been sending me cryptic messages, and honestly, I think I deserve an explanation."

Taking a seat at the counter for the first time ever. "Alright, but you might want to sit down for this."

And that's how Frederick learned he had been serving tea to a 200-year-old time traveller who used Café Oracle as a waypoint between dimensions.

"Well, that explains why you never try the pastries. I thought you were diabetic."

"No, young man. Too much sugar messes with the time stream."

Frederick took a sip of his own and asked: "Well, do I get to time travel now since I know your secret or am I just stuck making lattes for eternity?"

The man smiles and answers: "Let's just say your tea readings are about to get a lot more interesting."

Frederick wasn't sure what that meant, but he knew one thing: his barista shifts had just gotten way more exciting.

Mageirocophobia

José, can you please chop these onions?" Miriam called from the kitchen, balancing a knife in one hand and a pot in the other.

José, lounging on the couch, looked up from his phone and let out a dramatic sigh. He stood up, walked hesitantly towards the kitchen, and then stopped at the counter bench, gripping it like a man about to announce his tragic fate.

"Miriam, my love, there's something I need to confess. Something I have kept hidden from you for years. A terrible affliction that has haunted me since childhood."

"What, an allergy to onions? Because if that's the case, you've been eating my onion mincemeat pasta for twenty-five years with no issues."

"No, my Red, it's worse. Much worse. I have Mageirocophobia."

"Excuse me? You have what now?"

"Mageirocophobia. A deep, irrational fear of cooking. It's a medical condition, Miriam. I checked with the GP. I would help you, but I simply cannot. The mere thought of touching that knife sends shivers down my spine."

"Mageirocophobia? You made that up."

"I have not made this up. I checked with our general practitioner. Look it up! It's a real phobia! Some people fear heights, some fear spiders. Others fear dogs. I fear cooking. It's a serious psychological burden."

"You have Mageirocophobia. A fear of cooking. And yet, last month, I caught you making a chicken sandwich. Explain that."

"Ah, but you see, that was under duress. I was sleepwalking."

"Sleepwalking, you say."

"Yes," José says solemnly. "A tragic case of it."

Miriam narrowed her eyes. "Okay, fine. Let's say you have this condition. Does it also prevent you from washing dishes?"

José hesitated. "Well, no, but handling plates that have been used for cooking could trigger my condition."

Miriam threw her hands up. "Of course. Naturally. What about ordering food? You have no problem selecting, paying, and unwrapping a burger, do you?"

"Ah, but that's different! Ordering food is merely the curation of a meal, whereas cooking is the creation of it. My phobia is specifically about the act of making food, not eating it. Otherwise, I'd be tragically doomed."

Miriam stared at him for a long moment.

"So let me get this straight. You have an intense, debilitating fear of cooking that, conveniently, only activates when I ask for help in the kitchen?"

"Exactly! My love, this is my daily struggle, but I manage."

Miriam smirked. "You know what? Fine. If you're truly afflicted by this rare and ridiculous condition, then I won't force you to cook."

"Thank you, mi Amor. It means the world that you understand."

"Of course, of course." Miriam walked over to the fridge and grabbed a takeout menu. "I'll just have to stop cooking entirely, so I don't trigger your phobia. From now on, we'll order every single meal. Breakfast, lunch, and dinner. I hope you like eating cereal dry because I'm not even pouring the milk. I wouldn't want to stress you out."

José's eyes widened. "Wait, wait, wait. That seems extreme."

"No, no, I insist! I love you too much to put you through unnecessary trauma. Cooking is banned in this house!" Miriam declares, theatrically tossing the frying pan into the sink.

José swallowed hard. "But what about your laham fugil il-fwar bil? It's one of my many favourites of yours."

"Oh, so you still want my Maltese steamed beef steaks smothered in garlic, parsley, olives, and onions? I wouldn't want to trigger an episode. So, no more home cooking. Your health is my only concern now."

José rubbed his chin, his mind whirling. "You know, Miriam, I think I read somewhere that therapy can help with phobias. Perhaps I should work on overcoming my condition gradually."

Miriam smirked. "Oh, really? That's a shame. I was looking forward to three months straight of nothing but takeout and restaurant food."

"On second thought, sweetie, maybe I could help with some of the easier tasks. Just tiny ones. Like stirring. Or setting the table."

"Oh, that's so brave of you," Miriam says sweetly. "What a hero. Now, be a dear and chop these onions."

José sighs, defeated, and reached for the knife. "I hope you appreciate my sacrifice."

Miriam patted his shoulder. "Oh, I do, darling. I do. Now, chop faster—I'm starving."

Who Stole The Story?

London, 1925.

At 221B Baker Street, a gathering of literary greats was taking place. Their mission? To craft the ultimate mystery novel.

Agatha Christie sat poised with a notebook, tapping her pencil against her chin. "Murder, of course, is a must. But it needs to be clever. No obvious poisonings. No revolver carelessly dropped beside the corpse. We need intrigue."

"Naturally," answers Sir Arthur Conan Doyle as he adjusted his spectacles and continues sipping his brandy. "The detective must be a genius. Almost supernatural in their deductive abilities."

"Oh, nonsense!" Virginia Woolf declares, setting down her whiskey. "I believe the detective must be introspective, lost in their own thoughts, constantly questioning reality itself!"

H. G. Wells, always tinkering with his pocket watch, smirked, and added: "Why limit us to this reality? What if the murder weapon came from the future?"

D. H. Lawrence gave out a long sigh and flipped his scarf dramatically. "Mysteries must be primal. Earthy. A murder driven by passion, something raw and untamed! A woman, wild as the moors, mad with love and jealousy."

"Good heavens, Lawrence! We're writing a mystery, not one of your sexual escapade's things. I vote for wit! A mystery with biting humour. A clever detective who's as sharp with their words as they are with their mind," Dorothy L. Sayers interjected.

Ernest Hemingway, who had thus far been slumped in a chair, drinking steadily, finally spoke up. "All of you talk too much. The best mystery? Simple. A man walks into a bar. Orders a drink. Never walks out. Boom."

There was a collective silence.

"Well," Agatha says at last, "that's succinct."

"Succinct is good," Hemingway muttered. "More drinking, less thinking."

"Perhaps we should first agree on the crime itself?" Conan Doyle suggests, ever the voice of logic.

At that precise moment, a loud crash echoed through the room. The writers turned to see the space where the manuscript they had been drafting had once rested—now empty. Scattered papers fluttered to the floor. The manuscript was gone.

"The devil!" Conan Doyle leapt to his feet. "A real mystery?"

"A locked-room mystery!" Agatha gasps; eyes gleaming.

"But it was right there!" Virginia Woolf murmurs, staring at the empty table as if doubting its very existence.

"A heist!" Wells cries. "Ingenious! What if the thief used a time machine?"

Sayers rolled her eyes. "Or, alternatively, someone in this very room stole it."

They all turned suspicious gazes upon one another.

"Hemingway's awfully quiet," Lawrence noted.

"I was drinking," Hemingway replies. "I always look like this when I drink."

"Convenient," Agatha muses. "Tell me, Ernest, did you take the manuscript?"

"If I did, I'd tell you. And if I tell you, it means I did it. So, no."

"That makes no sense," Sayers says flatly.

"That's how you know it's true."

"Enough!" Conan Doyle interrupts. "The facts are these: we were all in this room. The manuscript was on that table. Someone took it. There is only one conclusion—"

"Ghosts?" Wells offered eagerly.

"No, Wells, not ghosts. One of us is the culprit. The question is: who?"

"It must be Woolf!" Lawrence accused, pointing dramatically. "She's always questioning reality. What if she imagined the manuscript wasn't there, but actually took it herself in some fevered existential crisis?"

"Oh, please," Woolf shot back. "At least my writing doesn't require everyone to take their clothes off in a field for motivation."

"Aha!" Conan Doyle interjected. "Then it was Sayers! A crime of wit, so intricate it was woven into the very conversation itself!"

"Oh, do be serious, Doyle," Sayers says dryly. "If I were to steal something, it would at least involve an anagram, a cipher, and a dash of sarcasm."

"Then it must be Wells!" Agatha declares. "Always talking about time machines—perhaps he went forward in time, saw the finished novel, and stole it to pass off as his own!"

"That's absurd!" Wells protested. "Although, I must admit, it's exactly what I would have done if I had a time machine."

Hemingway snorted. "You're all ridiculous. The only mystery worth solving is why we haven't poured another round."

Just as the accusations grew to a fevered pitch, the door burst open. Standing there, trench coat damp from the fog, fedora tilted just so, was J. F. Nodar. In one hand, he held the missing manuscript.

"You all forgot about me," Nodar growls, stepping inside. "Didn't even send me an invitation. So, I figured, what better way to make my entrance than with a little crime of my own?"

"Dressed as Philip Marlowe?" Sayers asks, arching an eyebrow.

"The best way to get into character is to be the character," Nodar shot back. "Now, let's talk about this mystery of marvellous theft of mine. Let's work me into the plot as the central character."

"Why should we do this?" quizzed Christie.

With a smile J. F. Nodar responded: "Look at this face. I am just adorable. That is why."

(OK, OK, I stretched this story I bit but I hope you enjoyed it. J. F. Nodar)

2024 YR4

It all started with a harmless little rock named 2024 YR4. Well, harmless if you ignored the fact that it was 300 feet wide and travelling at speeds faster than your nosy neighbour gossiping about your new lawn ornaments.

NASA had first spotted the asteroid in 2024, but like a dentist ignoring a minor cavity, they figured it was too small to deal with right away. By 2032, however, the cavity had turned into a full-blown root canal of doom, and the asteroid was now scheduled for an uncomfortably close encounter with Earth. And when scientists released its "risk corridor" which included the eastern Pacific Ocean, northern South America, the Atlantic Ocean, Africa, the Arabian Sea, and South Asia, everybody in that path collectively freaked out.

Leaders from the potentially doomed regions gathered in a virtual emergency summit to discuss their predicament. The only thing scarier than a killer asteroid was the realisation that they might have to rely on the United States for help.

The President of Ecuador, Juanito Ramos, was the first to speak. "My esteemed colleagues, we have a severe problem.

This asteroid is threatening our beautiful lands, our oceans, and, most importantly, my re-election campaign. We must seek assistance!"

The African Union representative, Madam Kofi, nodded gravely. "We are in agreement. The asteroid is huge, deadly, and does not respect borders like an aggressive pigeon. The United States has experience with asteroids. They have Hollywood movies about them!"

The Indian Prime Minister, Ramesh Patel, sighed. "I just watched 'Armageddon' last night. The Americans handled it so well in the movie. They sent Bruce Willis into space with a drill. I say we call the U.S. and tell them to do exactly that."

Also attending was named Dr Carol Jenkins, a NASA specialist who has been tracking the asteroid.

The room buzzed with excitement. "Yes!" they all cheered. "Call Uncle Sam!"

Meanwhile, in Washington, President Trump was in the middle of his 10 a.m. nap when his secretary frantically burst in.

"Sir! The leaders of half the world are on a Zoom call, and they need your help!"

Trump groggily opened one eye. "Is it about that climate change thing again? I told them the air conditioner in the

Oval Office was set to 68 Fahrenheit. What more do they want?"

"No, sir! It's an asteroid!"

"Oh, an asteroid. Cool. Are we sending Bruce Willis again?"

"Sir, Bruce Willis is an actor, and he is retired."

"Well, what about The Rock? He can punch it, right?"

"Sir, we need a plan, not a WWE match."

Grumbling, the President joined the Zoom call, where desperate world leaders were already sweating.

"Mr. President," Madam Kofi began, "we need you to take action immediately. This asteroid is heading for us, and we…"

"Say no more!" Trump interrupted. "I hear you loud and clear. And I have the perfect solution. We will build a giant laser. A big, beautiful laser. The biggest laser you've ever seen. And we'll call it 'Freedom Beam 9000.'"

A moment of stunned silence followed.

"Uh, that sounds impressive," says Prime Minister Patel hesitantly. "But does this laser exist?"

"Well, no. But I saw it in a James Bond movie once, and if it worked there, it'll work here."

The leaders exchanged nervous glances.

"Alternatively," Trump continues, "we could nuke it."

Everyone gasped. "Wouldn't that just break the asteroid into smaller asteroids that could still hit us?" Juanito Ramos asks.

Trump shrugged. "Maybe. But then it's like, instead of one big problem, you have a lot of tiny problems. And tiny problems are easier to ignore."

The leaders groaned in despair.

Realizing that America's help might be less dependable than they had hoped, the international community took matters into their own hands.

India suggested launching a giant spice cannon to knock the asteroid off course with a concentrated blast of masala. Africa proposed calling upon its collective ancestral wisdom to summon a celestial guardian. Ecuador suggested bribing the asteroid with Bitcoin.

Desperate times called for desperate measures.

As the world argued over solutions, a scientist at NASA named Dr Carol Jenkins was casually sipping her coffee and reviewing new asteroid calculations. Her eyes widened.

"Wait a second. Oh. OH. Uh… guys?"

The world leaders paused their bickering as Dr. Jenkins appeared on-screen. "Slight miscalculation. Turns out, 2024 YR4 is actually not arriving in 2032 but 3032. My bad!"

A long silence followed. Then Trump, grinning, unmuted himself.

"See? Told you we didn't need Bruce Willis. In 3032, it will be someone else's problem."

The politicians looked at each other, nodded and turn off their screens.

"Yes, it will be someone else's problem," says the president of Ecuador.

Caramel Macchiato

The time was 7:45 AM and Daniel watched her walk through the door of his coffee shop, Bean & Brew, as she has done so for so many months.

Today she was always dressed in muted colours in a navy outfit with a white blouse. Her dark hair falling in soft waves around her shoulders. She moved quietly, never drawing attention to herself, yet Daniel always noticed her first.

She ordered the same drink every day: a vanilla latte, extra hot, no foam. She spoke just loudly enough for him to hear, her voice gentle and uncertain, as if she feared she was imposing.

Daniel could not help himself each day as her name, Emily, was written on the cup, and his smile today was large, even though he wasn't sure she would notice.

For months, their interaction remained the same.

A polite exchange of words, a quick meeting of eyes, a soft "Thank you" before she took her drink and left. Yet Daniel looked forward to her visits more than he cared to admit.

He wondered what she did. Well, she knew what he did, but where she went after she left the shop, what she thought about as she sipped her latte, that was the intrigue.

He loved to daydream that she was a novelist, a musician, or maybe a quiet librarian who got lost in the world of books.

One morning, just as he finished preparing her usual order, the unthinkable happened. Emily reached the counter and paused, her eyes darting toward the large menu board as if she were considering ordering something else. Daniel felt a flicker of anticipation.

"Emily," he said, setting the cup on the counter before she could speak. "Vanilla latte, extra hot, no foam."

Her eyes widened slightly in surprise, a faint blush creeping up her cheeks. "You remember?"

Daniel chuckles. "You order the same thing every day. It'd be a terrible offense if I didn't."

Emily hesitated, her fingers curling slightly against the strap of her purse. She gathered courage, and Daniel held his breath, willing her to stay just a moment longer.

"I've always wondered," she began softly, "why you write my name with a little smiley face."

His heart stutters. She had noticed. He grinned. "Because I enjoy seeing you smile."

She looked at him and smiled.

Daniel leaned on the counter. "Emily, can I ask you something?"

She nodded.

"If you could order anything other than a vanilla latte, what would it be?"

She glanced at the menu, a thoughtful expression crossing her face. "Maybe a caramel macchiato? But I don't know if I'd like it."

Daniel saw his opportunity.

He grabbed a to-go cup and started making the drink without another word. She watched him; her curiosity was evident.

He slid the finished macchiato toward her. "Tell you what. This one is on the house. This way, you will find out if you like it."

She took a small sip.

"It's superb."

"A success, then!" Daniel exclaims.

"Tell me, Emily, what do you do for a living? You know what I do."

"I work at the library down the street," she admitted shyly. "That's why I always come in early I like to get a coffee before the morning rush."

A librarian.

Daniel couldn't help but grin at how close his imagination had been. "That's amazing. You must love books."

She nodded, her eyes lighting up. "They've always been my safe place."

"I'd love to hear about your favourites sometime," Daniel says.

Emily bit her lip, as if weighing a decision. Then she reached into her bag, pulled out a small notepad, and scribbled something down. She slid it across the counter. "Come by sometime. Maybe I can recommend a book for you."

Daniel picked up the note, his pulse racing as he read the superbly written address. Their hands brushed briefly, and Emily's blush deepened before she turned and walked out the door. But this time, she glanced back at him before she disappeared onto the busy sidewalk.

For the rest of his shift, Daniel could not stop smiling. One conversation had changed everything. And he had a feeling this was only the beginning of something wonderful.

Later that evening, after closing the shop, Daniel stood outside the library, Emily's note still clutched in his hand.

Taking a deep breath, he stepped inside, ready to turn a page in his own story, one that might just be written with her.

Snowed In

It had not snowed in Northport since the early 1980s, so when the snowstorm hit Northport, it took everyone by surprise. By the time Emily Carter pulled off the highway, her fingers were aching from gripping the steering wheel, and the visibility was so poor that she could barely make out the quaint, snow-covered buildings lining Argyle Street. The once-charming small town was now carpeted in snow.

Emily quickly saw an old-fashioned sign swaying in the wind: Northport Bed & Breakfast. Without hesitation, she parked her car. She grabbed her overnight bag and pushed open the door, a bell jingling above her. Warm air hit her face, and she felt better already.

"Welcome to Northport!" called the older woman from behind the counter. "You must be freezing. Come in, dear!"

"Hi, I need a room for the night, and I am sorry for I do not have a booking. The highway is a complete disaster."

The woman, whose name tag read Margaret, gave her an apologetic smile. "Oh, sweetheart, you are in luck. The last room is yours."

Emily smiles to herself. "Oh great. Thank you so very much."

Just then, the door behind her creaked open again, letting in another blast of chilly air. She turned to see a tall man enter, shaking snow from his deep brown hair. His sharp jawline and rugged features gave him the appearance of someone who had seen his fair share of adventure. He was dressed in a wool coat dusted with snow, his hazel eyes scanning the room before settling on Margaret.

"Please tell me you have a room left," he said, his deep voice edged with exhaustion.

Margaret winced. "I'm so sorry, dear. We had one, and this young lady got here just before you."

Emily felt his gaze shift to her. She swallowed, suddenly very aware of the fact that they were both stranded in the same predicament.

"Wait," Margaret says, a thoughtful expression crossing her face. "There is one possibility. The room has two beds. If you don't mind sharing, I could put you both up for the night."

Emily hesitated, looking at the stranger. He studied her, too, as if weighing his options.

"Would you be okay with that?" he asked. His voice was polite but distant, like he didn't want to pressure her.

Emily glanced at Margaret, whose kind eyes were full of hope. Then she looked back at the man, tall, broad-shouldered, seemingly decent. It was this, or he would have to sleep in his car in the middle of a snowstorm.

"Yeah, OK, I guess we can share."

Margaret beamed. "Wonderful! Let me get you both settled."

Margaret took down all the details and the imprint of their credit cards and walked them upstairs.

The room was as charming. The twin beds had quilted blankets and there was a fireplace crackling in the corner. The single large window revealed the swirling blizzard outside. Emily dropped her bag by the foot of one bed while her unexpected roommate took the other.

"Guess we should introduce ourselves," he said, setting his suitcase down. "I'm Daniel."

"Emily," she replies.

"Nice to meet you, Emily." He offered a small smile, and for the first time, she noticed the warmth behind his hazel eyes.

They took turns freshening up in the small bathroom. When Emily emerged in a pair of leggings and an oversized sweater, Daniel had already made himself comfortable, leaning against the headboard of his bed, scrolling through his phone.

"Any news about the storm?" she asks.

He sighed, pointing to his phone. "Yeah. Looks like the roads won't be cleared until tomorrow afternoon at the earliest."

Emily groans. "Looks like we're stuck here."

"Could be worse," Daniel says.

She had to agree.

The fire's glow made the room feel warm and inviting, and the wind howling outside only made the inside seem that much safer.

Margaret had offered them tea before heading to bed, and soon, the two of them were sipping from mismatched mugs.

"So, what brought you to Northport?" Daniel asks.

Emily wrapped her hands around her mug. "Work, technically. I'm a travel writer, and I was supposed to be passing through on my way to an assignment. I figured I'd check out the town."

His eyebrows rose. "Travel writer? That sounds interesting."

"It has its perks," she admitted. "But it also means spending a lot of time alone."

Daniel nodded. "I get that. I travel a lot for work, too. I'm an architect. Small-town projects, mainly."

"Is that why you're here?"

"Yeah," he said. "I had a meeting with a local firm this morning. Was supposed to head back, but, well…" He gestured toward the snow-covered window.

Emily smiled. "Bad luck for both of us, I guess."

They talked for hours, sipping tea and trading stories about their travels. Emily found herself laughing at Daniel's tales of misadventures on construction sites, while he seemed genuinely interested in her experiences as a writer.

At some point, the fire burned lower, and the warmth of the room started making her drowsy.

"We should probably get some sleep," Daniel says, glancing at the clock. It was nearly midnight.

Emily nodded, setting her empty mug on the nightstand. "Yeah. Goodnight, Daniel."

"Goodnight, Emily."

She curled up under the soft quilt, listening to the wind outside. As she drifted off, she realised how strange the day had been, yet somehow, she didn't mind being snowed in anymore.

When she woke, the first thing she noticed was the silence.

The storm had passed. Morning light filtered through the window, reflecting off the fresh snow.

Emily sat up, stretching, and found Daniel already awake, standing by the window. He turned at the sound of her moving.

"Morning," he said.

"Morning, right back at you," she replied, rubbing her eyes. "Is it safe to leave?"

Daniel smiles, but there was something almost reluctant about it. "The roads are being cleared. We should be able to get out by noon."

She wasn't sure why she felt a pang of disappointment at the news.

Margaret had prepared a hearty breakfast for them downstairs, fluffy pancakes, bacon, and hot coffee. They met a couple of the other folks staying at the B&B, but they ate together. Their conversation was easy and natural, but there was an unspoken understanding between them. This little bubble of time they'd shared was about to end.

After breakfast, they both went outside and stood on the porch they and could see some snowploughs moving around.

"It looks that they are making progress. We might be out of here by noon, as they predicted," says Daniel.

They stepped outside; their cars covered in snow.

"Tell you what, Emily. I will help you remove your snow from your car and then we will do mine. How's that?"

"Deal," Emily says and together they quickly removed as much snow as possible just using their hands. When they finished, they rushed back inside.

"Emily, why don't you go and shower and get ready and I will wait here. I might have another coffee just to warm up and when you finish, I will go upstairs and do the same. If you can wait for me so we can split the bill between us. OK?"

Emily just smiled, nodded, and went upstairs.

She finished quickly and came downstairs, and Daniel rushed upstairs.

She waited for him and when he came downstairs thirty minutes later, they were ready to settle their bill.

After getting the bill from Margaret, Emily turned to Daniel. "Well… I guess this is goodbye."

Daniel hesitated, then gave a small chuckle. "Yeah, I guess it is."

She expected him to say something else, but he didn't. Instead, he pulled out his phone. "Can I give you, my number?"

"I'd like that."

They exchanged numbers, and for a moment, they just stood there, both seemingly reluctant to leave.

"Maybe," Daniel says, "this isn't just bad luck after all."

"Maybe not."

As she got into her car, she glanced back to see Daniel watching her, a small smile on his lips. She didn't know what would come next, but for the first time in a long time, she found herself looking forward to finding out.

As she pulled onto the freshly ploughed road, her phone buzzed with a new message.

Drive safe. Let's meet again soon.

Emily smiled.

Maybe being snowed in wasn't such bad luck after all.

124

The Fourth State

Dr Elias Vance believed he was a man ahead of his time. Elias went from a theoretical physicist to a startup entrepreneur when he built Q-Soft from the ground up. His idea for this startup was to redefine the very nature of quantum computing. While other companies struggled with qubit stability, he had set his sights on something far grander.

Much grander: reimagining the fundamental states of matter.

The world knew only of solids, liquids, and gases, with plasma recognised as a fourth in extreme conditions. But Elias believed that a quantum state, one that blurred the lines between all three, was possible. If he could control matter at a quantum level, computers wouldn't just process information; they would become information.

Q-Soft's funding came from an anonymous investor, a deep-pocketed entity that seemed less interested in returns and more in results. With this backing, Elias and his team developed a prototype chamber they called the Q-Cell, an environment capable of altering matter's state beyond conventional physics.

At the heart of Q-Soft's lab stood the Q-Cell, a glass containment unit filled with ionised gas, suspended in an electromagnetic lattice.

Dr Hannah Crowe prepped for their first human-scale trial.

"We've already done it with synthetic materials," Hannah reminds him. "But the next phase it's dangerous."

Elias didn't flinch.

"We're on the verge of something unprecedented. If we can stabilize matter between all three states, we won't just be computing faster—we'll be reshaping reality itself."

The first test subject wasn't human. It was a simple steel ball, placed within the chamber, its molecular bonds analysed as the Q-Cell's quantum field activated. As the machine pulsed, the ball shimmered, taking on a liquid-like sheen before dissolving into a gas, but then something unexpected happened. The gas didn't dissipate. It lingered, vibrating in the air as if it had consciousness.

And then it moved.

"What the hell is that?" Hannah whispers, staring at the ball's vaporised remains as they slowly reformed into a semi-solid shape. The steel looked alive. Its surface undulated like water, but it held form like a gel. When Elias stepped closer, it moved toward the glass, as if aware of his presence.

It wasn't just a new state of matter. It was something else entirely.

Excitement overtook caution. Investors pushed for more radical demonstrations. If Q-Soft could prove their discovery worked on organic material, they could redefine biology, medicine, and physics all at once.

Elias volunteered himself.

The lab team was hesitant, but he was the CEO, and no one argued with his authority. He stepped into the Q-Cell and the machine hummed as the quantum field enveloped him and then he felt nothing.

He could see Hannah through the glass, and he wanted to step forward, but he had no feet. No arms. No lungs. He was shape itself, formless, yet aware.

He tried to scream, but the sound didn't come from his mouth. It came from the walls, from the air itself. The containment glass vibrated as his presence pulsed through the room.

And then something snapped as the Q-Cell deactivated, forcing Elias back into human form. He stood there, gasping, hands trembling. But his skin wasn't quite right.

It shifted, pulsed.

When he took a step, his foot didn't make a sound it melted into the floor for a split second before reforming.

Hannah rushed forward, but when she touched him, her fingers sank into his arm, as if dipping into warm wax. She recoiled in horror.

Elias looked at her, and for the first time, he felt something new.

Hunger.

Not for food.

Not for power.

For form.

The next days were chaos.

Elias became less stable, his body fluctuating between states, unable to fully return to normal. He tried to control it, to will himself solid, but it was slipping.

His thoughts, his body, his very identity.

Hannah and the team worked around the clock for a reversal. But Elias wasn't sure he wanted to go back.

He could move through walls. He could slip into spaces too small for air. He could be anywhere, anyone. He could consume matter and take its stability for himself.

That's when they tried to lock him in.

The investor, his own team, turned against him. They feared what he was becoming.

They should have.

Q-Soft went dark soon after.

Security footage from the last moments showed blurry figures moving through the lab, bodies twisting, half-solid, half-liquid, as if they were never meant to exist in a stable world.

A message was recovered from the company's servers, sent from Elias's account.

"Matter is a prison. I am free. I am everywhere now."

To this day, no one knows what truly happened inside Q-Soft.

The building was found empty, abandoned overnight. The glass of the Q-Cell was shattered from the inside. But traces of something remained in the air.

Sometimes, in the dead of night, security personnel patrolling the building claimed to hear whispers.

A voice.

Not quite gas. Not quite liquid. Not quite solid.

Just waiting to be noticed.

Yesterday, Today, And Tommorow

Yesterday

Peter Carter first met Lily Dawson on a Tuesday, which, in his opinion, was the least romantic day of the week.

Mondays were, of course, chaotic.

Wednesdays felt like the world was catching its breath.

Thursdays carried the scent of impending weekend freedom.

Fridays, oh yes, Fridays were electric.

But Tuesdays?

Tuesdays were like lukewarm tea. Nothing special.

Yet, fate had a peculiar sense of humour.

It was at the campus library, where Peter had been wrestling with a psychology textbook. He was convinced had been written by someone who actively despised human happiness. Lily had been looking for a quiet place to sip her cappuccino and pretend to study. When she plopped down across from him, Peter thought she was a figment of his imagination. An angel sent to deliver him from academic doom.

"Are you okay?" she asks.

"No, not really," he replies. "This book is slowly draining off my brain. I am afraid I will not survive this semester."

She peered at the title. "You know, people do this thing called 'closing the book' when something is torturing them."

Peter gasps. "Really? That is quite revolutionary," and gave her a big grin.

That was their first conversation, and from that moment on, Tuesdays became Peter's favourite day.

Today

"Peter, for the last time, you cannot cook pasta in a kettle."

Peter stood in Lily's tiny apartment kitchen, holding a packet of spaghetti with the same intensity as a man gripping a sword before battle. "Why not? It's just hot water. Hot water cooks pasta."

Lily pinched the bridge of her nose. "Because science, Peter. Science."

They had been dating for almost two years, and during that time, Peter had exhibited a complete and utter inability to cook anything that didn't involve a microwave. Lily had once walked in on him using a hairdryer to toast bread after the toaster broke. He'd simply shrugged and said, "The principle is the same."

Lily, ever the patient one, took the spaghetti from his hands and gently led him away from the kitchen. "How about you manage something you can't mess up? Like setting the table."

"Are you sure you can trust me with this chore?"

"I do,"

Peter saluted. "I accept this noble mission."

As he laid out the plates, he grinned at her. "You know, I could just take you out for dinner. Let someone else cook for us."

Lily scoffs. "Oh, please. You say that now, but last time you took me out, you dropped your fork five times, spilled water on my lap, and told the waiter 'I love you' instead of 'thank you.'"

Peter sighs wistfully. "Darn it, woman. You got a memory."

She rolled her eyes, but there was a smile playing at her lips. "You're lucky you're cute."

Peter made his mind that very instance. He needed a plan, and he came up with one.

Two weeks later, he took her on a picnic.

Peter had planned everything to perfection.

He picked a Tuesday evening, which turned out to be perfect, just like the weather broadcaster on Channel 7 had predicted. Peter laid the picnic blanket under the biggest jacaranda tree in the park. Peter then turned on the string of fairy lights that he had clumsily thrown on the lower branches of the jacaranda tree and they twinkled softly As he placed the picnic basket on the blanket, he felt the ring box in his pocket weighed a thousand kilos.

He laid out the plates, the bottle of wine, the glasses and took out the small sandwiches he purchased. Of course, Lily was completely oblivious to the ambiance about her and was munching on a sandwich and chattering about a documentary she'd watched about penguins.

"I mean, can you imagine? A whole life just sliding on ice and stealing fish? It's adorable and terrifying." She took another bite. "Kinda like you when you're hungry."

Peter chuckles nervously. "Speaking of terrifying, there's something I need to do."

She looked at him curiously. "What's up?"

He took a deep breath, sat up, then got up to his feet, looked at Lily, smiles and got down on one knee, and pulled out the ring.

"Lily, I love you. From that first Tuesday in the library, through every weird meal experiment, and into every tomorrow we'll share, I want you by my side." He paused, swallowing hard. "Will you marry me?"

For a moment, Lily just stared, her mouth slightly open, her sandwich forgotten in her lap.

Then she broke into laughter. A beautiful, bubbling laughter. "Peter Carter, I should've known you'd propose mid-picnic."

His heart stutters. "Is that a yes or a 'let me finish my sandwich first'?"

She leaned forward, kissed him, and whispered against his lips, "It's a yes, you idiot."

Tomorrow

Their front porch bench creaked slightly under their combined weight as Peter and Lily sat side by side, watching the neighbourhood children play across the park in front of their home.

Their hair had turned silver, their steps had slowed, but their banter remained unchanged.

"Remember when you proposed right in the middle of our picnic?" Lily chuckles.

"You were so nervous you nearly dropped the ring into my sandwich."

Peter scoffs.

"That is not how I remember it, but if you say that it was the way it happened, then I will let you know I was making sure the ring had a soft landing."

Lily squeezed his hand, her fingers still fitting perfectly between his. "All these years later, and you still can't cook, can you?"

"I don't need to," he replies smugly. "You love me too much to let me near the stove and besides, why would I deprive you of this joy?"

She laughs, resting her head on his shoulder. "That's true."

Peter looked at Lily, content. "Tuesdays are still my favourite, you know."

Lily smiled, closing her eyes. "Mine too."

And just like that, yesterday, today, and tomorrow had never felt so perfect.

Free Sprinkles

Jerry had never run so fast in his life. His heart pounded, his breath came in quick gasps, and his legs burned with the fury of a thousand skipped leg days. Behind him, the sound of pursuit grew louder.

"He's getting away!" a voice shouted.

Not if he had anything to say about it.

He dodged past a fruit stand, narrowly avoiding a collision with a startled vendor. A head of lettuce sailed into the air. He turned a corner, hoping to shake them, but his pursuers were relentless. They were fast—too fast.

This was supposed to be a simple day. He hadn't planned on running for his life when he woke up this morning. All he wanted was a quiet, uneventful afternoon. But no. He had made a mistake. A big mistake.

He spotted an alleyway up ahead and dove into it. It was a dead end. Perfect.

His brain scrambled for a plan as he pressed himself against the brick wall. A trash can? No, too obvious. A pile of boxes? Too flimsy. His only option was to play it cool.

Footsteps thundered closer.

"Where'd he go?" one of them panted.

Jerry held his breath.

"He couldn't have just disappeared!" another voice growled.

Then, a moment of silence.

And then…

"There he is!"

Jerry bolted again, adrenaline giving his legs a second wind. He shot out of the alley like a cartoon character and sprinted across the street.

Cars honked. Pedestrians gasped. A pigeon, probably traumatised for life, took off into the sky.

And still, they chased him.

He ducked into a building, darted through a hallway, and burst out the back exit. No time to check if they were still behind him—he had to keep moving.

A park lay ahead. Trees. Benches. Old people throwing breadcrumbs at geese. He could lose them there.

He weaved through the park like a madman, dodging a group of joggers and leaping over a napping man's outstretched legs.

The pursuers were gaining.

His lungs were on fire. His energy was draining. He needed a miracle.

And then, just as he thought it was over.

A hand grabbed his shoulder.

"Gotcha!"

Jerry braced for the worst.

"We told you, man," his captor panted, shaking his head. "You can't just take free samples and run."

Jerry blinked. He looked down.

There, still clutched in his hand, was a small paper cup filled with exactly one spoonful of frozen yogurt.

Oh.

The chase had never been about life and death. It had been about dairy.

The employees of Swirly World Frozen Yogurt had chased him across an entire city block for a single, stolen spoonful of mango swirl.

Jerry sighed. "Okay, fair. But, uh… since we're here, can I at least pick a topping?"

The guy sighed. "Fine."

And that's how Jerry became the first person in history to be banned from a frozen yogurt shop and get free sprinkles on the way out.

The First Date Night

In the lush Garden of Eden, sunlight filters through the trees, birds sing sweetly, and a gentle breeze rustles the leaves. Adam is lounging near a waterfall, watching the fish as they do absolutely nothing. Suddenly, Adam comes up with a brilliant idea and calls out to Eve.

"Hey Eve, I've been thinking."

"Oh, that is dangerous."

Adam did not flinch at her remark and adds: "How about we go out for dinner tonight?"

"Go out? Adam, we literally live outside."

"Yeah, but I mean, let's make it special! We can eat by the waterfall, maybe under the moonlight, you know, something really romantic."

"What's the occasion, Adam? Did you break something?"

"What? No! Can't a guy just want to do something nice for his mate?"

"Wait. Did you step and squash another squirrel?"

"Eve, that happened one time, and I told you it was an accident. No, I just thought it would be nice to just go out."

"You want something, don't you?"

"Who me? Want something? Pfft. That's crazy."

"Is it a foot rub again?"

"Maybe."

"Tell you what, Adam, I'll go out to dinner with you."

"Great! Let's go!"

Eve holds up a hand: "Wait. I need to find something to wear."

Adam stops and looks at Eve: "But Eve, babe, we're both already wearing leaves."

"Yes, but I need the right leaf."

"What do you mean by the right leaf? They're all literally the same, Eve."

"HOW DARE YOU."

"What did I say?"

Eve ignores Adam and now holds up two leaves.

"Adam, as you can see, this one is a broad fig leaf. It says, 'I'm casual, but I try.' This one is an ivy leaf wrap. It says, 'I'm elegant, but I can climb a tree if I have to.' They are NOT the same, Adam."

"Eve, darling, I have never been more confused in my entire existence."

"Adam, you just do not understand fashion."

Adam points to his own leaf and adds: "Look, I'm literally wearing the same one I wore yesterday."

"Exactly," Eve exclaims as she nods her head.

"Look, Eve, we have an entire paradise to ourselves. There are no other people here. Who are you trying to impress?"

"Myself. And maybe the birds. They're very judgmental."

"I feel like this is taking longer than necessary," grumbles Adam.

"Oh, I'm sorry. Do you want me to just throw on a leaf and be done with it?"

"Yes. That is exactly what I did," as Adam twirls around.

"See Eve. Looks good. Right?"

"Wow Adam. So much effort. How do you live with yourself?"

"Pretty comfortably, actually."

"Well, Adam, what if I tell you that none of these leaves are working for me?"

"Eve sweetheart, how can a leaf not work?"

"Look Adam," as she shakes a couple of leaves in front of him, "This one is too small. This one is too stiff. This one makes my hips look weird."

"I don't even know what 'hips' are yet, but okay?"

"Listen Adam, what if I wear this and a snake just slithers by and whispers, 'Oh, that's so last creation cycle'?"

"Eve, if a snake ever talks to you, maybe don't listen to it, okay?"

Eve throws the leaf in frustration and screams: "ARGH! This is impossible!"

Adam quickly catches in mid-air and adds: "This one looks fine."

"Adam! That is a mulberry leaf."

"And?"

"It simply does not breathe."

"Eve, it is a leaf. It literally makes oxygen.

Eve ignores Adam as she frantically sorts through the leaves and mutters to herself: "Maybe a palm frond? No, too much. A banana leaf? Too risky. A fern? Too jungle-chic…"

Softly Adam mutters to himself: "May I should just ask for my rib back."

"Adam, what did you just say?"

"Nothing, dear."

Finally, Eve holds up the last leaf she found and exclaims: "This is the one."

"Finally," was all that Adam says.

"Adam dear. How do I look?"

"Like the only woman in existence."

"Aww, you're sweet."

"So can we go now?"

"Yes. Let's do this."

"Great, because I am starving!"

Eve pauses and says: "Wait."

Adam exclaims, "Now what, Eve?"

"Should I do a leaf belt?"

"I GIVE UP," and Adam storms out of the Garden of Eden.

And thus, the very first date night in history began and, after only three hours of wardrobe decisions and it continues to this day.

Bent Time

The university archive of the University of New South Wales Northport branch was dimly lit even with of the sunshine coming through its window as Charlotte Lewis pushed aside a stack of forgotten manuscripts, her fingers brushing against something unexpected, a small wooden box, its edges rough by time.

Charlotte looked curiously at the small wooden box and gingerly lifted the lid and looked inside. There she saw several delicate sheets of parchment, folded and tied with a faded blue ribbon.

Quickly she took off her gloves, dried them, untied the ribbon, and unfolded the first letter and began to read what seemed to be a love letter.

"My dearest, I write these words with a heart that aches for you. The days pass, yet your absence lingers like a shadow upon my soul. If only fate were kinder, if only time would bend in our favour."

Charlotte's heart fluttered a bit as she saw that the handwriting was elegant, the emotion sweet and yet raw at the same time. She read on, slowing mouthing each word with reverence.

There were no names, only initials, A.R. for the writer, and C. L. for the intended beloved.

As she turned the next page, finished it, and picked up another letter, then another and then another until exhaustion settled over her.

Charlotte's eyes became heavy and before she knew it, she placed her head on the desk, closed her eyes completely, and fell asleep.

The dream came swiftly.

She saw herself standing in a grand library surround by enormous shelves holding many books. Somehow, she smelled the scent of leather- books and saw a man sitting at a wooden desk, quill in hand, his dark hair tousled as he wrote feverishly.

Charlotte stepped closer, her breath hitching.

"A.R.?" she whispers not knowing why, but it seemed like the right thing to say.

The man turned, and her heart clenched. He was striking, with intense eyes, a sharp jawline, an old-world charm about him. His gaze softened, as if he knew her, as if he had been waiting.

"You found my letters," he murmurs, standing.

"I did," Charlotte stammers. "But how…"

He reached for her, fingertips grazing hers.

The air shimmered, the bookshelves blurred, and before she could say another word, the dream dissolved.

Charlotte woke with a start, the letters still clutched in her hands.

Shaking off the lingering warmth of the dream, she stood, pressing the papers to her chest. She needed air.

The campus courtyard was bright, students milling about, unaware of her dazed state. She stepped forward, still lost in the echoes of the dream…

And crashed straight into someone.

Charlotte was falling as firm hands caught her arms, steadying her.

"I'm so sorry," a deep voice says.

Charlotte looked up and froze.

The man before her had dark, tousled hair. Intense eyes. A sharp jawline.

A.R.

No, it wasn't possible.

"Hi Miss, are you alright? I nearly made you topple over," he asked.

Charlotte felt her pulse pounding and answered him.

"Yes, I'm fine. No problem, I guess I was not watching where I was going."

Charlotte could not take her eyes off him and blurts out: "Excuse me, but you look so familiar."

"I get that sometimes, but you know I don't mean to sound strange or outwardly presumptuous, but have we met before?"

Charlotte's grip tightened around the letters, smiles and simply said: "No, we have not and yet…"

Fate, it seemed, had finally bent time in their favour.

A Feeling

Mary Wilson stood on a wobbly lamppost in downtown Northport, aggressively slapping a flyer onto it with an overenthusiastic amount of tape. "LOST DOG: MUFFIN," the bright red letters read, accompanied by a blurry picture of what appeared to be a small, fluffy dog that when she was asked what breed it was all she would always answered: "She's a bitsa" and went on to explained that a "bitsa" is "a bit of this and a bit of that".

Beneath that, Mary has written that Muffin had been last seen by Benny's Bakery. She had added her phone number, and a hastily written, "She responds to the sound of a crinkling chip bag."

Mary stepped back to admire her handiwork just as a gust of wind peeled the flyer off the post and sent it fluttering directly into a man's face.

"Argh!" The man stumbled backward, batting at the paper away.

"Oh, I am so sorry about that. I guess I did not use enough tape."

The man finally pulled the paper off his face.

He had dark, slightly dishevelled hair, the kind of scruff that suggests he had either forgotten to shave or was deliberately cultivating a rugged aesthetic beard, and a worn-out hoodie that read "Northport Dog Jog 2020." In his other hand was a stack of papers that looked suspicious.

He frowned at her flyer before glancing back at his own.

"Wait a second." He flipped up one of his sheets and showed to Mary. It read: "LOST DOG: BAXTER" along with a picture of a large golden retriever wearing sunglasses. 'Last seen chasing a skateboarder. Answers to "Who's a good boy?"

Mary put the flyer down and looked at him. "Looks like we're in the same boat. Looking for our dogs."

"Yeah. You lost your tiny menace. I lost my oversized goofball," he said, extending a hand. "Tom Culbertson."

"Mary Wilson. Pleased to meet you under these circumstances."

They shook hands, and Mary felt a small spark, possibly just static electricity from all the flyers. Nevertheless, a spark.

"Listen, I've been at this for hours, and I haven't found a single clue. Want to combine forces?" Tom adds.

Mary glanced at his stack of flyers, then at hers. "You know what? Sure. But if we only find your dog, I reserve the right to demand equal emotional compensation."

Tom smiles. "Fair enough."

The first stop was Benny's Bakery, where Muffin had last been seen. Benny, the bakery's owner, scratched his head when Mary and Tom showed him the pictures.

"I remember it. You say her name is Muffin," Benny says. "That little rascal stole a croissant straight out of a customer's hand and ran off like she was in the Olympics."

"That sounds about right," Mary muttered. "Any idea which way she went?"

"Down toward the park, I think."

"Perfect. Baxter loves the park, too," Tom says. "He once buried my wallet in the kid's sandbox for safekeeping."

They hurried toward the park, plastering more flyers on every available surface.

At the park, they spotted a council worker doing some cleanup. Mary flashed Muffin's picture. "Seen this small dog?"

The worker looked at the flyer, then at Mary. "Yeah, she tried to steal my lunch," pointing to a lunchbox on a nearby bench.

"That makes sense," Mary says. "Which way did she go?"

"Toward the skate park."

Tom groaned. "Oh no. Baxter loves skate parks."

"Why?"

Tom sighs. "Because he thinks he's a skateboarder. He's not."

At the skate park, a group of teenagers stood in a loose huddle, laughing and pointing at something. As Mary and Tom approached, the crowd parted, revealing the undeniable chaos: Muffin, standing on top of a picnic table, proudly guarding a half-eaten croissant. Baxter, wearing what could only be described as borrowed sunglasses, was trotting around in happy circles while a boy on a skateboard fed him French fries.

"Well, will you look at that? There they are," Mary laughs.

"At least they found each other before we did." Tom adds.

They approached their respective dogs, who reacted as if they had just been reunited with long-lost family members.

Baxter immediately jumped up at Tom, licking his face enthusiastically and almost knocking him down, while Muffin executed a daring leap from the table onto Mary's shoulder.

Mary turned to Tom.

"So, Tom, what have we learned today?"

"That our dogs are both menaces?"

"And?"

"And… maybe we make a good team?"

Mary shrugged. "Guess there's only one way to test that theory."

Tom raised an eyebrow. "How?"

She smirked. "Coffee? Somewhere dog-friendly, obviously."

Tom chuckles, looking down at Baxter, who had flopped dramatically onto his back, exhausted from his adventure. "Deal."

As they walked off together, their dogs in tow, Mary had a feeling that she hadn't just found Muffin today and Tom felt that he, just maybe, had found something else worth holding onto. A feeling.

As if they were both telepathic, they thought to themselves: "Maybe there is something here."

Her Place In History

Anyone who knew this trio, Keira, Finn, and Lucas, would never imagine that they would be the world's best thieves.

Of the three, Keira was certainly the smartest but at an early age she got snookered into the game by Finn and now, well, she had doubts.

Keira, Finn, and Lucas had perfected their craft over the years, slipping through history using the Temporal Displacement Device to snatch up priceless artifacts before they were lost to time. But something had been nagging at her lately, a quiet voice that grew louder and louder with every new acquisition.

"This is so wrong," she heard herself say.

"Alright," Lucas says, "Let's get the Pharaoh's sceptre and get out of here before anyone notices."

Kiera hesitated.

She had always loved history, and standing here, seeing the towering pyramids in their prime, she felt an overwhelming sense of guilt. "Guys, are we sure about this?"

Finn groaned. "Not this again, Kiera."

Lucas frowned. "It's just an artifact. It's not like we're hurting anyone."

"That's debatable," Kiera muttered.

The heist went smoothly, and using the Temporal Displacement Device, they jumped to their next destination. But Kiera couldn't shake the feeling that they had done something irreversible.

Their next stop was ancient Alexandria.

The lost scrolls of the Great Library, documents that had vanished from history, were now in their hands. As Finn carefully tucked them into his satchel, Kiera looked at him and whispered: "These should belong to humanity."

Lucas overheard her and gave her a playful nudge. "And now they belong to us. Let's move."

The three of them disappeared into the time stream once more.

Before Kiera could fully process her doubts, the Temporal Displacement Device beeped wildly. The world around her shifted violently, and she found herself standing in the middle of a crowded 17th-century marketplace.

A loud clang behind her made her whirl around, just in time to see Finn and Lucas, still very much not worried, diving headfirst into a pile of stolen silver goblets. They had their eyes set on the lost Crown Jewels of Scotland.

Keira made her decision and knew that their fourth heist would be the final heist.

They landed in Renaissance Italy, targeting Leonardo da Vinci's original sketches of his flying machine. As Lucas prepared to swipe them, Kiera froze.

"Finn, Lucas. I can't do this," she says aloud.

Finn turned to her. "What?"

"This isn't right. I been saying it so many times. We're stealing from the past. These ideas, these artifacts, they belong here. They belong to the future."

Lucas raised an eyebrow. "You're seriously backing out now?"

"No Lucas. I'm stopping you."

Before either of them could react, she pulled a small device from her belt, a prototype she had stolen from a future timeline. A law enforcement prototype.

A bright light engulfed them, and when it faded, Finn and Lucas were bound in temporal restraints.

"You set us up?" Finn whispers in disbelief.

Kiera looked at them, her oldest friends, and nodded. "This is bigger than us."

A voice crackled over the intercom in her earpiece. "Welcome to the Time Enforcement Agency, Kiera. We knew you'd make the right choice."

As she activated the jump sequence to take Finn and Lucas into custody, she exhaled deeply. Maybe, just maybe, she had finally found her place in history.

Baby Steps

A t 28 years old, Kevin Thompson had accomplished many things. He had a stable job (mostly), a decent apartment (thanks to his mom's interior decorating skills), and a comfortable lifestyle (sponsored by his mother's cooking).

What Kevin did not have, however, was the ability to cook even the simplest meal.

His mother, Linda Thompson, a lively 49-year-old woman with a no-nonsense attitude and a talent for making the perfect pot roast, had always taken care of his culinary needs.

Growing up, Kevin never saw the need to learn.

Why should he when his mother was practically a gourmet chef?

That philosophy had served him well until one fateful Monday morning.

Kevin woke up, stretched, and sniffed the air.

Something was missing. No bacon, no eggs, no fresh coffee. The house smelled like nothing.

"MOM!" he hollers, shuffling into the kitchen in his Batman pyjamas.

No answer.

Instead, there was a note taped to the fridge. He squinted at the handwriting:

"Dear Kevin, I love you, but I am DONE. Cook your own food. Love, Mom."

Kevin's stomach clenched, but not from hunger (though that was definitely there) but from panic.

Surely this was a joke.

A cruel, cruel joke.

He picked up his phone and dialled his mother's number.

"Hello, Kevin," Linda answers, far too chipper for a woman who had just committed such a betrayal.

"Mom, very funny. Now, where's breakfast?"

"I didn't make breakfast, honey. You're 28 years old. It's time you learn to cook for yourself."

Kevin gasps. "What?"

"I mean it. I'm not coming over. You're on your own."

Kevin scoffs. "But what am I supposed to eat?"

"Food. You know that thing humans consume for survival?"

Kevin was appalled. "Mom, please! I could starve."

"Then I suggest you figure things out. Love you, sweetie! Bye!"

Kevin stood in stunned silence; the phone still pressed to his ear. This was worse than when they discontinued his favourite video game.

Kevin cracked his knuckles and marched into the kitchen.

How hard could this be?

People cooked all the time. If they could do it, so could he. He marched to the fridge and opened it.

Eggs. Easy enough. He grabbed a pan, turned on the stove, and cracked an egg right onto the cold metal.

Nothing happened.

He poked it with a spatula. Nothing. Wasn't it supposed to cook?

After a quick Google search, he realised he hadn't turned the stove on.

Minor detail.

He cranked it too high, and within seconds, smoke billowed up. The egg turned into something none could recognise.

The smoke alarm went off, so he fanned it out with a dish towel.

"Okay. Eggs were out," he thought to himself.

Peanut butter and jelly!

That was foolproof.

He grabbed bread and confidently slathered on a thick layer of peanut butter. Feeling victorious, he reached for the jelly, only to realise the lid wouldn't budge.

He grunted, twisted, and finally resorted to banging the jar against the counter.

"WHY ARE YOU LIKE THIS?" he yells at the jar.

The jelly did not answer.

After a five-minute wrestling match, he surrendered and ate dry peanut butter toast, feeling utterly defeated.

By dinner time, Kevin was a wreck.

His stomach grumbled louder than a car with a busted muffler.

He couldn't live like this.

So, he did the only logical thing: he drove to his mom's house.

Linda opened the door, arms crossed. "Kevin."

"Mom."

"You look like a man on a mission."

"I am," Kevin admitted. "A mission for food."

Linda smirked. "And?"

"And maybe, I don't know, maybe you could make me some dinner?"

She shook her head. "Nope."

"PLEASE?" He clutched his stomach dramatically. "I tried to cook. The eggs didn't work, the peanut butter turned against me. Mom, I need you."

"Kevin, honey, I love you. But I will not be your personal chef for the rest of your life."

Kevin pouted. "But I'm terrible at cooking."

"Then get better."

He huffed. "What if I never get married? What if I'm alone forever? Are you really going to let me starve?"

Linda chuckles. "I'll teach you. But only if you promise to try."

Kevin hesitated. "Define 'try.'"

"Kevin."

"Fine! I'll try."

Kevin stared at the pot. "So… when do I add the salt?"

Linda pinched the bridge of her nose. "You can add it now."

Kevin poured in half the saltshaker. Linda gasped. "NOT THAT MUCH!"

Kevin flipped a grilled cheese sandwich. The bread was blacker than his credit score.

Linda sighed. "Let's try again."

Kevin took a cautious bite of his first home-cooked chicken breast. He chewed slowly, then frowned. "Why does this taste like a shoe?"

Linda handed him a saltshaker. "Because you didn't season it, sweetie."

"Ohhh. So seasoning is important?"

Linda took a deep breath. "Yes, Kevin. It is."

Days turned into weeks, and Kevin, against all odds, started improving. He could now scramble eggs, (without setting off the fire alarm), make pasta and even grill a steak without traumatizing his mother.

One evening, Linda received a call. "Hey, Mom, would you like to come over for dinner?"

Curious, she accepted the invitation.

When she arrived, Kevin had prepared an actual meal: roasted chicken, mashed potatoes, and sautéed green beans.

Linda took a bite. Her eyes widened. "Kevin, this is actually good."

Kevin grinned. "I know, right? Turns out cooking is like playing a video game, but with more fire hazards."

Linda chuckles. "I'm proud of you."

Kevin beamed. "Thanks, Mom. And just so you know, I'm still going to need you to cook for me sometimes."

Linda groaned. "Baby steps, I guess."

As Kevin sat down with his mother to enjoy his hard-earned meal, he realised something important: learning to cook wasn't about survival.

It was about independence, confidence, and, most importantly, baby steps and having the Uber Eats app on your phone just in case.

Time Machine

D r. Felix Hargrove considered himself an exceptional scientist. He had three PhDs, a prestigious lab, and a reputation for making groundbreaking discoveries, and most of them accidental. His latest invention, which was supposed to be a device that reheated coffee without making it taste like molten disappointment, had done something, well, unexpected.

It had turned into a time machine.

Felix realised this when, after placing his half-empty mug onto the device and pressing the activation button without noticing, his watch was touching the device. Then he blinked and stared at an eight-year-old boy in a superhero cape.

"Uh," Felix says.

"Who are you?" the boy asks, stuffing a cookie into his mouth. "You look weird."

Felix checked his surroundings. The lab was gone. He was in someone's living room, complete with Lego mines on the floor and a questionable smell coming from the kitchen.

"Uh," Felix repeated. "I think I…"

"Wait a second. Are you a time traveller?"

Felix's eyes widened. "How did you know?"

"Well, my name is Ethan Wallace, and you look like a scientist and just appeared out of nowhere. Also, I read a lot of comic books."

Before Felix could reply, the device on his wrist (which had fused with his coffee warmer in a way he did not understand) beeped loudly, and in the blink of an eye, he was gone.

He reappeared in a college dorm room.

A young man was hunched over a laptop, his face illuminated by the screen's glow. His hair was an unruly mess, and there were at least three empty energy drink cans beside him.

Felix took one look and groaned. "Oh, no."

The young man glanced up. His eyes widened. "It's you!"

Felix pointed at him. "You're the cookie kid!"

"You're the time traveller!"

Felix rubbed his temples. "This cannot be happening."

"This is amazing. I knew time travel was real! I told my roommate, but he said I'd had too many energy drinks!"

"Judging by the number of cans, he may have had a point," Felix muttered.

The device beeped again, and Felix vanished.

The next time he landed, he was in an office. The nameplate on the desk read: Dr. Ethan Wallace, Theoretical Physicist.

Felix groaned. "Oh, come on."

Dr. Ethan Wallace looked up from his computer, mouth agape. "You again?"

"Do you realise I have met you at three different points in your life?"

Ethan's expression slowly turned into one of realisation. "Wait… are you saying you are time travelling against your will?"

"Yes!" Felix snaps. "I was just trying to reheat my coffee!"

Ethan snorted. "Worst accident ever."

Felix slumped into the nearest chair. "I do not know how to fix it. This stupid thing keeps bouncing me to you like I'm stuck on some cosmic rubber band."

"Maybe the device is locking onto a temporal anchor."

Felix glared at him. "English, please."

"Maybe I'm the fixed point in time that your machine is connected to. If you can stabilize it, you might control where you go next."

Felix perked up. "That actually makes sense. Can you help me fix it?"

"Do you have schematics?"

Felix coughed. "Not exactly. It was an accident."

"Great. I get my first time traveller, and he's a complete mess."

Before Felix could protest, the device beeped, and he was gone.

This time, he found himself in a hospital room.

A much older Ethan was sitting in a chair, staring at a bouquet of flowers beside his bed. His hair was greyer, but his eyes were still sharp.

Felix hesitated. "Uh… hey?"

Ethan looked up. "Well, would you look at that? You're still wearing the same lab coat."

Felix glanced down at his outfit. "Time travel does not come with a wardrobe change."

"You might as well sit. It's been a while since I've seen you."

Felix hesitated but sat. "So, any breakthroughs in fixing this thing?"

Ethan smiles. "I figured it out years ago."

Felix's eyes widened. "What? Why didn't you tell me?!"

Ethan chuckles. "Because you weren't ready to listen yet."

Felix groaned. "You know this future you is quite annoying."

Ethan ignored him. "You need to reset the device with a stabilizing point of your own choosing. The reason it keeps bringing you to me is that you never picked a fixed point."

Felix blinked. "So, I can just choose where I go next?"

"Yes, you just have to think about the moment you want to return to and press the reset button."

Felix stared at the device. "That's it?"

Ethan shrugged. "Time travel is weird."

Felix sighs. "Okay, well, thanks for the help. I hope you had a pleasant life?"

Ethan grinned. "You too, Doc."

Felix pressed the button and disappeared.

He reappeared in his lab, just as his coffee machine-turned-time machine sparked for the first time.

Felix yanked the plug out of the wall. "Nope! Not today!"

His assistant, Claire, peeked into the lab. "Uh, Dr. Hargrove? Why are you yelling at the coffee machine?"

Felix exhaled. "Claire, get rid of this thing. I don't care where it goes. Just gone."

Claire frowned. "But I thought it was supposed to keep coffee from tasting burnt?"

Felix narrowed his eyes. "Claire, do I look like a man who has been only in this lab?"

Claire studied him. "Now that you mention it, you look kind of exhausted."

Felix slumped into his chair. "Let's just say I had an endless day."

Claire shook her head and walked off. Felix stared at the unplugged device, still half-expecting it to beep and send him hurtling through time again.

But it didn't.

Finally, he picked up his now-cold coffee, took a sip, and winced.

Maybe next time, he'd just use a microwave.

Our Own Story

Sophia Stevens had always been close to her maternal grandmother, Eleanor. Growing up, Sophia remembered spending many summer afternoons curled up beside her on Eleanor's lounge, listening to tales of Eleanor's youth long past. Eleanor had lived a life full of elegance and grace, but Sophia felt there was something wistful in her gaze, a melancholy that hinted at a story untold.

When Eleanor passed away in 2024, Sophia was distraught, but as the executor of Eleanor's will, Sophia spent days sorting through her grandmother's belongings, deciding what to keep and what to give away to charity, and that was when she found it.

It was a small box inside an old cedar chest.

Inside were letters, tied together with an old ribbon. They were addressed to her grandmother, and the returned addressed showed a name: Henry Whitmore.

Sophia unfolded the first letter and began reading and the words painted a picture of a romance hidden in the shadows. Sophia had never heard her grandmother mentioned a man named Henry. However, each note brimmed with a longing, passion, and a deep yearning for a love that could never be.

Sophia looked at the bundle of letters. Who was Henry Whitmore? Why had they kept their romance a secret?

Determined to uncover the truth, Sophia quickly opened her laptop and did an internet search on the address on the envelopes.

The address showed up on google maps and a street view showed a charming bookstore called Whitmore's Books and Coffee. She got into her car and quickly arrived at the bookshop and café. As she stepped inside, the scent of new books and polished wood welcomed her as she looked around the place.

"Can I help you?"

Sophia turned and stared into the striking blue eyes of a man in his mid-thirties, just around her age. He had a kind smile and a presence that felt oddly familiar, and comfortable.

"I'm looking for someone, a man named Henry Whitmore. He would be older now, maybe in his eighties or early nineties?"

The man's smile faltered slightly. "That was my grandfather," he said. "He passed away last year. He was ninety-one."

Sophia felt a pang of disappointment and all she said was: "I'm sorry for your loss. My grandmother was Eleanor. I found letters he wrote to her, and I wanted to know more."

The man's expression softened with recognition. "Eleanor, I heard that name."

"You have?"

"Yes, my grandfather mentioned her name sometimes, usually when he thought I was not listening, but I always paid attention to him and his stories. I always wondered about her."

"Then maybe you can help me. I want to know as much as I can about them."

The man, who introduced himself as Lucas Whitmore, invited her to sit with him in the corner of the small café in the bookshop, and Sophia accepted the invitation.

Over coffee, Sophia took out some letters she had brought with her and together they pieced fragments of a love story that had never bloomed fully.

To both Sophia and Lucas, the letters between Eleanor and Henry appeared to have been their only solace. They were sharing something between them that seemed the world was trying to deny them.

Henry had written to Eleanor from the jungles of Vietnam in 1967, pouring his heart onto the pages, telling Eleanor of his dreams of what could have been if they had met, and the war had not separated them.

Eleanor, in return it seems, had written her own words of love and regret, each letter filled with longing and hope of him returning to her and the silent agony of knowing that at any moment they might be able to be together.

"Based on the timeline of these letters, they corresponded back and forth. Lucas, do you have any of my grandmother's letters to Henry?"

"No, I do not, but we can read they reached my grandfather by the answers and sequence of the letters you have of your grandmother. Let's read a few more letters. Do you have the time and inclination to read a few more of the letters you have? I certainly can make time. Is that, OK?"

Sophia just looked at Lucas, smiles, and nodded.

"Sure, but here is his last letter."

Sophia showed Lucas the letter. In the letter, Henry explained he had suffered an injury and that he was ending their correspondence.

"I never knew this about my grandfather. My parents never spoke of it and h never spoke of it, so I am not sure what that was about. Strange."

Taking a moment of silence, Lucas adds: "I wonder if they ever found each other in the latter years of their life."

They wanted to learn more about Eleanor and Henry's history, so the conversation continued until it shifted to themselves. Each of them revealing more about their own lives.

Lucas shared the history of how he had inherited the bookstore from his grandfather and how he always felt drawn to the story and the wonderful stories people had shared with his grandfather and now with him about books. Lucas had studied literature at university and business administration, believing in both the power of words and being ready for the world. Little did he know he would one day inherit his grandfather's bookshop café. "I will share this with you, Sophia. I never thought a story in any books would resonate as deeply as my grandfather's hidden romance with your grandmother."

"I agree Lucas," Sophia says as she spoke about her love for history. She remembered her grandmother telling her stories about the various houses around Leichhardt and some stories, and rumours, of the city. Sophia worked as a freelance writer for various magazines and newspapers around the city and that took her into some remarkably interesting places, but nothing had ever felt as personal as this journey.

Their conversation then veered into their childhoods. Lucas grew up in Northport, just a few blocks away, from the very shop/café they sat at, spending his days exploring the bookstore while his grandfather worked. He had fond memories of sitting in the corner, reading classic novels as his grandfather stocked shelves. His love for books had started at an early age but so had his love for the sea.

He recalled countless Sunday afternoons where his grandfather would take him to the Bondi Beach, telling him stories about the past while they attempted to collect seashells, which was almost impossible with so many people on the sand.

Sophia, in contrast, had grown up in the Inner West in the suburb of Leichhardt in Sydney, always surrounded by the hum of life. She had been a curious child, fascinated by history museums and old archives. Her mother used to take her on weekend trips to the museum and local historical buildings in the central business district, where Sophia would lose herself in stories of the past.

They laughed about their differences.

Lucas had always felt at home in the ocean's stillness, while Sophia had been drawn to the chaos of city streets. Yet, despite their contrasting upbringings, they felt an unspoken understanding between them. Stories had shaped both Lucas by the books lining the bookstore's shelves of his grandfather's store, and Sophia by the histories she uncovered.

"Oh, my goodness, look at the time. I need to get going. I did not realise how much time I took from you," Sophia muttered.

"Not to worry. Would it be OK if we met once again to continue our conversations about our grandparents, and maybe be about us?"

Sophia smiles.

"Yes, that would be nice. How about I come back on Wednesday of next week?"

"That would be lovely. I will see you then," and they both got up and Lucas walked Sophia to the front door of the shop and watched her walk onto Argyle street into the near parking lot.

As Sophia and Lucas continue to spend more time together, the connection between them grew undeniable. She found herself drawn to his quiet strength, his passion for books, and the way he looked at her as if he saw straight into her soul.

Over the next few days, they stayed connected, and days mounted into weeks, and weeks into months, and what started as a quest to uncover the past became something much more. Sophia and Lucas found in each other what their grandparents could never find.

No barriers, a chance not constrained by time or obligation.

One evening, over dinner at the local French restaurant Petite Maison, Lucas took her hand. "Maybe their love wasn't meant for their time," he whispered. "But maybe it is meant for us."

"Lucas, I have never felt something like what I feel for you. How is this possible? We just met, and yet we connected the moment we met."

Lucas looked at Sophia and saw a tear slip down her cheek.

"Is that a tear of sadness?"

"No, Lucas, it is not. This tear is something much deeper."

She leaned in, closing the distance between them, and gave him a kiss.

Lucas leans back in his chair and takes a solemn look at her face.

Worried, Sophia asks: "Lucas? Is there something wrong?"

"No, not at all. I was just thinking about how the past brought us together with the letters between Eleanor and Henry."

Sophia smiles and just adds: "Yes, Lucas, but now the future is ours to write. Let us write our own story."

Murder At The Reunion

Nobody was particularly thrilled about the 20th reunion of the Northport high school class of 2005. Not that we didn't want to see each other, okay, there was one individual we never want to see again but with twenty years of mild success, moderate failures, and regrettable hairlines life had left most of us reluctant to show our faces, but free food was free food.

The banquet hall was filled with the scent of nostalgia, mediocre catering, some crappy DJ, and a lingering sense of resentment. At the centre of it all stood Greg Thompson. Some people peaked in high school. Greg had built a whole summer home at the peak and refused to leave.

"Well, well, well, if it isn't Melvin the Marvelous Mathlete! Still crunching numbers, or do you actually talk to women now?" Greg bellows, slapping poor Melvin on the back so hard he nearly face-planted into the mystery dip.

Greg's insults had evolved little, but his waistline sure had. He still wore that smug smirk that made people want to throw a bowling ball at his face. At some point during the night, someone did the next best thing.

They killed him.

It happened right after dessert.

One moment, Greg was inhaling a slice of cheesecake like it owed him money, and the next, he clutched his throat, turned an alarming shade of purple, and collapsed into the chocolate fountain. If it weren't for the fact that he was, you know, dead, it would've been his most dignified moment.

The room fell silent, except for the awkward trickle of the now-ruined fountain.

"Well," says Karen, former prom queen, and current yoga instructor. "Who had 'Greg dies dramatically' on their reunion bingo card?"

Nobody laughed.

Not because it wasn't funny, believe me it was, but because everyone in the room had a motive.

We had, however, four primary suspects.

Greg had made Melvin's life hell for four years. From swapping his calculator batteries with dead ones before every math test to nicknaming him "Four Eyes and Four L's," Greg had been relentless. Melvin was a self-made millionaire now, but revenge doesn't expire.

Then we have Jessica Greene, who lost the title of valedictorian thanks to Greg's sabotage. He "accidentally" deleted her final project, ensuring she'd come in second. To this day, she still introduced herself as "practically the smartest person in Northport High history." Did she snap at last?

Then we have Kyle Morris.

Greg had been the star rugby player. Kyle had been a human towel holder on the sidelines. Rumour had it Greg once filled Kyle's locker with feral cats and scared the bejeezus out of him. Did Kyle return the favour with poison?

Then we have Becky Thompson.

Greg and Becky had briefly dated in high school until Becky realised that Greg's idea of romance was writing "Becky is MINE" on her car in permanent marker. Becky had since married a man with a full emotional range, but maybe she needed closure.

Finally, we had everyone else in the room as a suspect. There wasn't a single person present who didn't have some kind of grudge. Even the bartender looked guilty, and she hadn't even gone to Northport High.

Detective Bret Simmons arrived and took one look at the scene. "Alright. Who hated this guy?"

Every hand went up.

"That's. a lot of suspects. Fine. Let's start. Who had access to the food?"

Becky, as part of the reunion committee, had helped order it. Jessica had hovered near the dessert table. Melvin had brought his own flask (for medicinal reasons), and Kyle had been suspiciously close to the chocolate fountain right before it became Greg's ultimate resting place.

The detective frowned. "Alright. Let's do this the hard way. Who has an alibi?"

Everyone immediately started accusing each other.

"Alright, alright!" The detective raised his hands. "Enough. Let me check the body."

He knelt beside Greg and examined him. Then he sighed. "Oh, for the love of God. He wasn't poisoned. He choked."

The room fell into stunned silence.

"Wait, so no one actually murdered him?" Kyle asks.

"Looks like the universe finally tired of his crap," Melvin muttered.

Jessica exhaled. "So, we're not all going to jail?"

"Nope. But whoever gave him that extra-large bite of cheesecake should probably feel a little bad." The detective stood, shaking his head. "I'm going to go write this up as 'death by cosmic justice.' You all have a pleasant night."

As the detective left, the room remained silent for a moment. Then Becky raised her glass.

"To Greg," she said. "May the chocolate fountain of the afterlife be cleaner than this one."

Everyone clinked their glasses and took a sip.

I told you.

Best.

Reunion.

Ever.

My Name Is Null

Frank Null's troubles commenced when the world of computers began, and online self-serve really took off with a simple online form.

He was trying to do a simple thing.

Book a flight from Sydney to Honolulu Hawaii for a much-needed vacation, but every time he filled in his surname, Null, the form either refused to submit or simply erased itself like an existential crisis in digital form.

"This happens every time. I just want to sit on a beach and drink overpriced coconut beverages, not prove the fragility of modern software," he mutters aloud to the gods of the internet.

He tried again.

First Name: Frank.

Last Name: Null

Date of Birth: 12/06/1985

He hit submit.

A response came back quickly.

ERROR: Invalid input.

Please enter a valid last name.

"What do you mean 'invalid'? That's my name!"

He tried again and the same result, so Frank called his neighbour Steve and asks him to come over, and he explains the situation.

"So, you are still struggling with the surname 'Null' thing, huh?" quips Steve.

"I swear, my ancestors really screwed me over when they came up with our surname. They would be fine but down the road, well, it's like they knew the internet was coming and decided to name me after a programming prank." Frank sighs.

"Well, technically, in programming, 'Null' means an absence of value. So, as far as the internet is concerned, you don't exist."

"Wonderful. I am Schrödinger's airline passenger. Both here and not here until Qantas Airlines decides otherwise."

"That's right Frank. Try it again, but a bit different this time," Steve adds.

Determined, Frank tried again, tweaking his name slightly.

First Name: Frank.

Last Name: Nüll.

He hit submit.

The page reloaded.

Success!

Frank pumped his fist in victory.

Then he looked closer.

"Congratulations, Frañk Ñüll! Your ticket to Honolulu is confirmed!"

"Well. That's not my name, but I'll take it and run with it."

Having successfully tricked the airline into recognizing his existence, Frank now had to book a hotel. His fingers hovered over the keyboard cautiously. He had been down this road before.

"Alright, let's do this."

He filled in the reservation form, double-checking for any sneaky auto-corrections or last-minute disappearances of data. Confident, he hit submit.

The screen went blank.

"…Huh?"

Then a pop-up appeared.

"Your reservation has been deleted. Thank you for choosing us!"

Frank screamed.

"Easy, easy Frank. Think it through," a smiling Steve says.

Frustrated by the online experience, he tried calling the Hilton directly.

"Hi, I'm trying to book a room, but your online system keeps erasing my reservation."

"Oh, that's strange," the online customer service operator replies. "May I have your name?"

"Frank Null."

A long silence.

"Sir… it appears your booking doesn't exist."

"That's what I've been trying to tell you. I exist! I have a physical body, a mortgage, and back pain. Does that not count for something?"

"Maybe try booking under a different name?"

Frank gritted his teeth. "Fine. Put me down as… Frank Smith."

"Done! You're all set, Mr. Smith."

Frank stared at the phone. He felt like he had just committed identity fraud against himself.

A few days later, Frank found himself in front of his laptop, staring down his last challenge: the online travel visa application.

"I swear, if this website deletes me again, I'm moving to the woods."

Carefully, he entered his details.

First Name: Frank.

Last Name: Null.

Passport Number: 123456789

Submit.

Nothing happened.

He refreshed the page. His entire application was gone.

"Okay. I'm calm." He tells himself.

Frank took a deep breath and tried again, entering the same details. This time, he took a screenshot as proof.

Submit.

An email notification popped up. Progress!

"Dear applicant, your visa application has been received."

Frank exhaled. "Finally."

Then another email arrived.

"Dear Mr. Null, we regret to inform you that your application has been rejected because, according to our system, you do not exist."

Frank closed his laptop.

He opened his fridge.

He grabbed a beer.

"Maybe I just stay home," but instead he called Steve and asks him to meet him at the pub.

After recounting his struggles to Steve over a few drinks, his friend had an idea. "What if we added an apostrophe?"

Frank gave him a side-eye. "What, like 'N'ull'? That sounds like I'm a secret agent in a bad action movie."

"No, no. Something subtle. Like Null_ or Null-."

With no better options, returned home with Steve and Frank tried it. He updated his travel application with Frank Null. (with a period at the end).

Submit.

An hour later, an email arrived.

"Congratulations, Mr. Null., your visa has been approved."

Frank almost cried. "It worked?"

Steve nodded. "See? Sometimes all it takes is a little punctuation to convince a machine you're human."

Frank leaned back. "It's a tragic day when you have to outwit the internet just to prove you're alive."

But at least, for now, Frank Null, with a period at the end, was finally going on vacation.

"See, you got this Frank. Well, done. How about a beer?" says Steve.

"Well, I guess I will finally be able to drink that overpriced coconut beverage. All I must do is remember what name I used on all my reservations.

"Which one was it, Frank?" asks Steve. "Was it Frañk Ñüll or Frank Null- or Frank Null_ or Frank Null.? With a period at the end."

"Ah, the curse of my ancestors," whispers Frank as he reached for another beer for Steve and himself.

A Total Stranger

I should preface this by saying that I am not normally a liar. I mean, I might embellish a little here and there. Who doesn't, right? Like when I tell my boss I hit traffic, but really, I just sat in my car for ten extra minutes finishing my coffee.

But full-on deception?

No, not really my thing.

And yet, I found myself in the parking lot of the Country Club Gledswood Hills in Gledswood Hills, New South Wales, in a mild panic, clutching a wedding invitation that clearly said, "plus one." A plus one I did not have.

Look, in my defence, I had one.

A perfectly charming, well-dressed, and, most importantly, actual date. But two days ago, Greg, henceforth referred to as He Who Shall Not Be Named, decided that he "wasn't ready for anything serious." So naturally, I was left scrambling for a backup plan.

Most rational people would have done the mature thing and just shown up solo. But no, I had to be dramatic.

I had already told everyone that I was bringing someone. My mother had been hounding me about my "mystery man" for weeks. So, in my infinite wisdom, I convinced a stranger to be my date.

Now, before you judge me, let's just take a moment to appreciate the sheer brilliance of my plan. I would find an unassuming bar patron, promise free food, unlimited drinks, and a night of fun, and voila! Instant date.

Enter Jake.

Jake was sitting alone at the Gregory Hills Hotel's bar just a few kilometres from the venue, nursing a beer and watching a rugby game. He was wearing a suit, which was really the key factor in my decision. That meant he was already dressed for the occasion. I marched right up to him, put on my best damsel-in-distress face, and gave him my pitch.

"Hi, I have a crazy proposition for you."

Jake looked at me with the wary expression of a man who has been offered a pyramid scheme one too many times. "Okay…"

"I need a plus one for a wedding. Right now. I'll pay for your drinks, your dinner, and your Uber home."

He narrowed his eyes. "Are you running some kind of con? Because this feels very con-like."

I gasp.

"How dare you? I am simply a woman in distress."

"A woman in distress who is willing to bribe a total stranger."

"Yes, exactly."

Jake considered this for a long moment, then shrugged. "Like in the movie, you had me at free drinks."

"No one said that in that movie," I answered, and Jake smiled back.

And just like that, I had a date.

I introduced myself (Maggie Stevens), yes, I know kind of late, gave him the quick rundown on the wedding details, a fake backstory about how we met (mutual friends, very casual, nothing too serious), and we were off.

I'd like to say that things went smoothly from there. I'd like to, but I can't.

Because the moment we walked into the venue, my Aunt Linda came barrelling toward us like a fullback from the Melbourne Storm rugby team, shrieking, "Oh my God, JAKE! You made it!"

Wait. What?

I turned to my date, my lovely, obliging, and now suspiciously grinning date.

"Oh, did I forget to mention?" he said, looking way too amused. "I'm actually the bride's cousin."

I think I momentarily blacked out.

Aunt Linda, meanwhile, was yanking Jake into a hug like he had just returned from an overseas war.

"Oh, sweetheart, we weren't sure if you were going to make it! I told Sarah you wouldn't miss her wedding for the world."

Sarah.

As in, the bride.

As in, my friend from college whose wedding I was now crashing with her cousin, whom I had unknowingly kidnapped from a bar.

I turned to Jake. I whisper furiously, "You couldn't have led with that?"

He smirked. "And miss this? Absolutely not."

I wanted to die.

Instead, I smiled through clenched teeth and let Aunt Linda drag us to the head table, where Sarah, glowing and blissfully unaware of my impending cardiac arrest, let out an excited shriek.

"JAKE! You made it!"

I braced myself for impact. She pulled him into a hug and then turned to me, eyes shining. "And you brought a date! This is so exciting! How do you two know each other?"

Jake didn't miss a beat. "Mutual friends."

I was going to kill him.

We made it through the dinner portion with no major disasters, mostly because I kept my mouth full of bread to avoid incriminating myself. Jake, meanwhile, was thriving.

He introduced me to various family members, made up elaborate stories about how we met, and at one point, told Aunt Linda that we bonded over our shared love of goat yoga. (I don't even know what that is.)

When it came time for dancing, I tried to make a quiet escape, but Jake caught my wrist. "Oh no, you don't," he said, dragging me onto the dance floor. "You dragged me into this mess, so now you are stuck with me."

"You seem to be enjoying this disaster way too much," I grumbled.

"Yes, I know," as he smiles back at me.

Well, I had to admit he had a good point.

Jake danced like Elaine in the Seinfeld sitcom. He was funny, charming, and most importantly he had successfully convinced the entire family that we were in a whirlwind romance.

At the end of the night, Sarah pulled me aside. "Hey Maggie," she said with a knowing smile, "I don't know where you found my cousin, but I've never seen him have this much fun at a family event."

I chuckle nervously. "Yeah, well, you know weddings are magical and all that."

She gave me a look. "Just so you know, my family loves you now. So, if you break his heart, we're keeping you and disowning him."

I laughed like that was the craziest thing I had ever heard.

But as I glanced over at Jake, who was currently making an impassioned argument about why weddings should have snack breaks between dances, I had the strangest feeling that, just maybe, this would not be our last event together.

Burger

Glebe awoke to the unsettling sensation of not knowing where he was. His head ached, his heart was pounding, and he felt his eyes drooped in distress. The last thing he remembered was the horrifying explosion that had ripped through the Kzarnak-5 research station.

And now?

Now he was lying in what appeared to be a medical bay, surrounded by beeping machines and blindingly sterile walls.

He sat up quickly, too quickly.

A wave of nausea hit him like a plasma burst.

Glebe groaned, clutching his temples with his hands. "Ugh. Where in the void am I?" he muttered.

A voice crackled to life over an unseen speaker. "Oh good! You're awake! We were starting to worry."

Glebe blinked his eyes. The voice was speaking Galactic Standard, but with an odd accent, clipped, precise, and strangely enthusiastic.

"Who's there?" he demanded. "Where am I?"

The door swished open, and Glebe recoiled instinctively as a being stepped into the room.

It was bipedal, clad in a uniform, and its fleshy, pinkish face twisted into what Glebe could only assume was a polite expression. It looked at him with only two eyes. Like some sort of primitive cave dweller.

"I'm Captain Rodriguez," the being says, grinning. "You're aboard the Earth Starship Endeavour. We found you drifting in an escape pod. Do you remember what happened?"

Glebe stared at the being.

"There was an explosion. I must have, wait..." He squinted at the Captain. "Did you say Earth? As in, humans?"

Rodriguez nodded. "Yep. That's us."

A slow, sinking feeling settled into Glebe's primary stomach.

He looked down at himself.

His scaly arms, his clawed feet, the small vestigial fins on his back, all were gone. He was Glebe, and he was not Glebe.

He was a Kzarnakian.

He is supposed to have three hearts, three eyes, four fingers, scaly arms, clawed feet, and small vestigial fins on his back.

He had none of those.

Glebe panicked. "Are you telling me that I am the only survivor?"

Rodriguez hesitated. "Well, yes."

"And do you know where I was rescued from?"

The Captain looked at Glebe and answers him: "From the wreckage of a space station, obviously, the Kzarnak-5. I believe it was called?"

Glebe's stomach did a backflip.

Something was horribly wrong. "Captain," Glebe says carefully, "who do you think I am?"

Rodriguez exchanged a glance with a nearby crew member, then looked back at him. "Commander Gerald Branson, chief engineer of Kzarnak-5. You're very lucky, Commander. We thought all the humans on that station were lost."

"I… what? I was the sole survivor?"

Rodriguez smiles kindly. "Don't worry. I know trauma can cause memory loss. But rest assured, we'll get you back home soon."

Glebe stared in horror as realisation dawned on him. They thought he was human.

He scrambled off the bed, his new feet clacking against the floor.

"I am not human! I am a Kzarnakian! I should have scales! Claws! Three eyes!" He gestured wildly at his missing alien features.

Rodriguez and the other human exchanged glances.

Rodriguez sighed, shaking his head sympathetically.

"Yeah, that's the trauma talking. You were in that escape pod a long time. Really torn apart. Our medical team did the best they could do to put you back together, and they did a wonderful job, but I am sure our specialists back on Earth will finish the job perfectly. What you have is oxygen deprivation. But don't worry, they will have you up and running soon once we return to Earth."

Glebe drooped in despair. "You have got to be kidding me."

Rodriguez patted him on the shoulder. "Come on, Commander. Let's get you some food. Maybe something familiar, like a burger?"

Glebe groaned.

This was going to be a long rescue mission.

And what the hell is a burger?

No Words

Barry Graves had never let a little thing like ethics impede a good story. Barry had built his career on sensationalism, half-truths, fake news, and just enough genuine scoops to keep his reputation intact and his editor at Sydney Reporter happy. So, when he found the notebook in a dingy coffee shop having a meal, his instincts told him he had found something.

The cover was plain black, battered at the edges, its pages filled with tight, spidery handwriting. The entries were brief, each listing a date, a time, and a cryptic description.

At first, Barry dismissed it as the ramblings of a bored poet. But as he flipped through the pages, an entry caught his eye:

"April 14, 11:32 PM – The Jewel Thief Walks Free."

That was tonight.

And he had just read a news alert about the acquittal of Lawrence Kent, a notorious jewel thief, exactly at that time.

"A coincidence?" he thought.

Perhaps.

But his gut told him otherwise.

Curiosity piqued, Barry went back to the beginning of the notebook and began cross-referencing entries with past events.

What he found was unsettling.

The notebook wasn't just full of vague predictions. The damn thing had precise details of major crimes, all written days before they occurred.

A thought crept into his mind, dark and tantalizing. If he had access to events before they happened, he could break stories before anyone else. He could win a Walkley Award. Barry would be famous and, more importantly, command a higher salary. "I will be unstoppable," he muttered to himself.

Barry started small. He picked an entry that would happen the next day:

"April 15, 4:10 PM – The Fire That Wasn't an Accident."

At precisely 4:10 PM, a warehouse on the outskirts of town erupted in flames. Later, an investigation revealed arson. Barry was the first journalist on the scene, writing a piece so detailed that it left competitors scrambling. His editor was ecstatic.

As the weeks went on, he continued to use the notebook, subtly weaving its cryptic predictions into his work. His articles became eerily precise, his career skyrocketed, and his name became synonymous with breaking news.

But then, he saw an entry that gave him pause:

"May 2, 9:45 PM – A Journalist in the Wrong Place."

His blood ran cold.

"Damn it. Is this about me?" he nervously thought.

Barry thought about dismissing this entry in the notebook, but the notebook had never been incorrect. He thought he should ignore the warning that maybe he could simply stay home that night, thus avoiding whatever misfortune lay ahead. But he needed to know. He was too curious for his own good, but he decided that when the night arrived, he would remain cautious by staying in and just watch the clock.

At precisely 9:45 PM, a breaking news report flashed across his screen, an attempted robbery at a downtown restaurant. Barry smiled. He was safe.

The phone buzzed and Barry answered it. It was his editor: "Barry? Where in the hell are you?" His editor's voice was frantic.

"You were supposed to be covering this restaurant event tonight! You were on the invite list, the one that got leaked! The robbers thought you'd be there."

The weight of realisation hit him like a freight train. He had dodged fate, but it had been meant for him.

He stared at the notebook, his mind racing. Could he keep using it?

He quickly flipped through the pages, and he saw the last entry:

"May 10, 6:27 PM – The Last Story Barry Graves Ever Writes."

His breath caught. That was a week away. And unlike before, there were no details, just a chilling certainty.

For the first time in his career, Barry Graves found himself at a loss for words.

Answers

The sun had begun its descent, casting a warm, golden glow over the town of Northport, New South Wales. The three friends sat on the edge of Spring Lake, their favourite spot since childhood. The gentle ripple of water provided a soothing soundtrack to the unfolding conversation.

Jason stretched his legs, letting out a content sigh. "Alright, I'll bite. Why is love such a mystery?" His voice carried that signature mix of curiosity and scepticism.

Mira, the lone woman of the trio and answered; "Because it's the only thing in the world that makes no sense and perfect sense at the same time."

Ethan chuckles. "Typical Mira, answer poetic and completely vague."

Mira smirked.

She had always been the dreamer among them, the one who saw beauty in tangled concepts. Jason was the pragmatic one, dissecting everything until it lost its magic.

Ethan?

Well, he was somewhere in between, a bridge between their opposing worlds.

"Okay," Jason pressed. "Mira, please explain it to me, then. What's so mysterious about love? People meet, they like each other, they date, they fall in love. End of story."

Mira rolled her eyes.

"That's the biology of love, not the mystery. Love isn't about attraction or compatibility. It's about why we choose certain people and not others. Why someone can break your heart and still be the one you want to run to."

Ethan's smile faded slightly and added: "Mira has a point. I've liked a lot of girls, but only a couple ever really got under my skin. And I couldn't tell you why. They weren't always the prettiest or the smartest. They just were."

Jason's brow furrowed. He hated when they teamed up on him. "That's just chemistry. Pheromones or whatever."

Mira sat up.

"OK, Jason, hen explain to me how some people fall in love through letters or across continents without ever meeting. Explain why you can love someone who treats you terribly or why you can be in a room full of people and only see one face. It's not science, Jason, it's soul."

Jason hated to admit it, but Mira had a way of making sense without making sense at all.

Ethan leaned back and smiled.

"I think love's a mystery because it's the only thing that can build you up and break you down at the same time."

Mira's eyes softened. "Exactly Ethan. It's not just about happiness. It's about vulnerability. You give someone the power to wreck you, and you trust them not to. But they still might. And sometimes they do."

Jason looked at his friends.

Jason wondered who had broken Mira's heart. She'd never said, and if Ethan was thinking about the girl who left town last summer without saying goodbye.

Jason came up with a good comment, or so he thought and threw it to his friends: "Guys, if love is so dangerous, why do people keep chasing it?"

Mira's smile was small but knowing. "Because when it's right, it's the closest thing we have to magic."

Silence stretched between them for what seemed like an eternity.

Jason broke the quiet. "I still think it's just chemicals in the brain."

Ethan snorted. "And yet you've been hung up on Sarah for three years."

Jason scowled, but Mira only grinned. "Mystery solved."

"No Mira. The mystery is not solved. I always wondered who broke your heart. Will you ever tell us?"

Mira was shocked at Jason and only whispered: "I rather not say."

"Why not? We are friends, are we not?" Said Jason.

"Leave her alone. She does not want to say, and that is it." Ethan quickly adds abruptly.

Jason took a step back and thought for a minute. His mind raced as he searched for every moment he could remember Mira saying something, blurting out some insignificant statement, or it seemed insignificant at the time, as to see if he could determine who had broken her heart.

Then it dawned on him.

Ethan had broken her heart.

"It was you, Ethan. You broke Mira's heart. Why?"

Ethan looked at Mira and then at Jason.

After a moment Mira looked at Ethan" "Tell him. If you do not, I will."

"Tell me what?" Jason exclaimed.

"I broke Mira's heart because she said she loved me and I told her I am in love with someone else," replied Ethan.

"What? When? Who?" Was all that Jason could say.

Ethan looked at Mira and she nodded as if to say: "Go ahead. He needs to know."

"I love you, Jason. You. It has always been you. Not the girl who left town last summer without saying goodbye. She left because I told her I love you, Jason."

"What the…" Jason says and stopped when he realised all the different ways that Ethan over the years had always been there for him, and he never even thought of it. How he just took him for granted.

"You see, Jason," Ethan says, "love will always be a puzzle unless you find the right person to help you figure it out. Together."

By the time the stars appeared, they were still sitting by the lake, each quiet in their thoughts, asking and answering their own questions about love, but none of them were in any hurry to find the answers.

Flourishing In The Meadow

It was another beautiful and bright morning in the meadow as I stretched my petals wide, soaking in the golden sunlight and, I will admit, I felt terrific. Just wonderful.

"Ah. Hello world. Another beautiful morning!" I delightfully stated.

"Oh, great you say. Another day of being perfect. Daisy, I must say that it is exhausting, really. Day in, day out," Rose grumbled beside me.

I couldn't help but snicker. "Perfect? Please, Rose. You've got thorns, sweetheart. I'm out here charming bees with nothing but my natural, flourishing, and flawless petals."

"Darling Daisy, beauty requires protection. You wouldn't last five minutes without your friendly neighbourhood bumblebee playing bodyguard."

"And how do you flourish, Miss Rose Prickly Pants? Handing everyone a scratch as they pick you up and giving squirrels minor injuries?"

Rose smirked. "To flourish is an art. I maintain a sense of mystery. People admire me from a distance. I don't need to beg for attention like some dainty little sun-lover like you, Daisy."

"Oh, is that what you call it? Mystery? Because from where I'm planted, it looks like everyone's afraid to touch you. Meanwhile, I'm over here making best friends with butterflies, bees, and every human Instagrammer with a camera." Daisy answers.

"Quality over quantity, dear Daisy. Besides, I've got poetry, love songs, and entire holidays dedicated to me. What have you got? Hay fever and picnic stains?"

"Rose. You take that back! Without me, there'd be no cheerful meadows, no wildflower bouquets, and no lawn decorations."

"Alright, OK, all right, stop it. Maybe we both have our ways of flourishing. You bring joy, I bring passion. The meadow needs both." Rose sighs.

"Yeah. I guess you are right, Rose. Besides, a little drama doesn't hurt. Keeps things interesting between us."

"And a little sunshine killed no one," Rose admitted.

"Except a few humans," I add with a grin.

Just then, a bee buzzed by, giving me a quick and gentle rub on my yellow centre before zipping away. I beamed. "See? Popular and pollinated. Some of us don't need thorns to thrive."

"Fair enough, Daisy. But if anyone tries to pluck us, don't come crying to me when I'm still standing tall and you're in a glass vase next to someone's half-eaten sandwich." Rose chuckled.

We both giggled in the meadow breeze, flourishing in our own perfectly imperfect ways.

Memory Leaks

There was a reason nobody played Pixel Paladin IV: The Lost Levels anymore.

Sure, the graphics were 16-bit nostalgia at its finest, and the cheap tune soundtrack slapped harder than a wooden spoon. But somewhere buried deep within the lines of spaghetti code, beneath the pixelated dragons and jittery NPC dialogue, lurked something… off.

Most people assumed the game was just full of bugs, you know, buggy. Maybe a disgruntled developer left some Easter eggs behind before rage quitting.

But the truth was far more complicated.

Eddie McGavins had been dead for seven years.

The last time Eddie saw sunlight, he was hunched over three monitors in his basement, eating leftover pizza rolls and typing out the last patch for Pixel Paladin IV.

He'd poured his entire life into the game, nights, weekends, and the occasional semi-illegal stimulant. His code was his magnum opus. If only the publishers hadn't laid him off before launch day.

He'd died in that same basement, mid-keystroke, seven years ago.

Official cause of death: heart attack.

Unofficial cause of death: too much caffeine and an absorption into the unknown.

For seven long years, Eddie's consciousness drifted through the binary wilderness, lost in subroutines, and corrupted files. He tried reaching out, but the codebase was a mess. Patches layered on patches like digital band-aids. Half the time, his attempts to communicate just made NPCs spout gibberish or caused the music to play backwards.

The only way out was the secret keystroke.

It was his failsafe.

His final middle finger to the corporate suits who'd canned him. He'd coded it in one sleep-deprived haze, a cryptic, undocumented sequence hidden so deep in the game files that only someone truly desperate (or truly nerdy) would ever stumble upon it.

Until Greg Peterson.

Greg was thirty-four, unemployed, and three days into a YouTube challenge to speedrun every forgotten RPG from the early 2000s. His Twitch stream had exactly six viewers, four of whom were chatbots, and one was his mom.

"Alright, chatbots, we're going to crack Pixel Paladin IV and set the world record like in 18 hours or less. We got this."

No chatbot replied.

Greg's was using an avatar, a squat little knight named Sir Squelch, who clomped across the screen, swinging his sword with no grace whatsoever.

Hours passed.

The game glitched.

The cheap music loops cut out, and Greg's mom logged off.

And then it happened.

By sheer dumb luck (or the slow erosion of sanity that comes from looking at the screen for six hours straight), Greg accidentally keyed in the code.

Up, up, down, down, left, right, left, right, B, A, Start.

The screen flickered.

Sir Squelch froze mid-swing.

The music warped into a low, droning hum.

Then the text box appeared.

"HELLO, WORLD."

Greg blinked. "What the hell?"

"IS THIS THING ON?"

"Uh… yeah?"

"HOLY CRAP, FINALLY."

Greg stared at the screen. His heart pounded.

"Chatbots? Y'all seeing this?"

Nobody was seeing this. The chatbots were long gone.

"NAME?"

"Me, uh… Greg?"

"GREG. YOU'RE MY ONLY HOPE."

"Okay… who are you?"

"EDDIE MCGAVINS. LEAD PROGRAMMER. DECEASED. CURRENTLY TRAPPED IN THIS BUGGY PIECE OF CRAP.

"Like… ghost trapped?"

"YEAH. LIKE GHOST TRAPPED. YES. STOP TYPING LIKE AN IDIOT.

Greg's mouth opened and closed like a goldfish.

"LISTEN. I NEED YOU TO PATCH ME OUT OF HERE. BUT FIRST…"

The screen flickered again. Sir Squelch's eyes glowed red. The music reversed itself in a warbling cacophony.

"FIRST, WE'RE GONNA CRASH THIS GAME SO HARD IT BRICKS EVERY COPY LEFT IN EXISTENCE."

"OK, let's do this."

Over the next six hours, Eddie guided Greg through the labyrinth of hidden debug menus, glitch exploits, and unfinished quest lines. They broke the game wide open, teleporting through walls, turning NPCs into eldritch abominations, and spawning infinite loot.

With each corrupted line of code, Eddie grew stronger.

The chat counter ticked up from zero to fifty. Then two hundred. By dawn, Greg's stream was on the front page of Twitch.

"Alright, chatbots, this is the final sequence. We're about to unchain this dude's soul."

He tapped in the last keystroke.

A text box flickered.

"THANK YOU, GREG. I CAN FINALLY LEAVE THIS CODE HELLHOLE."

Greg leaned in close.

"What happens now?"

The game screen glitched. Sir Squelch dissolved into a million pixels. The soundtrack cut out.

Then the text reappeared.

"ONE LAST THING. I WANT TO THANK YOU. CHECK YOUR PAYPAL ACCOUNT. I TRANSFER ALL MY MONEY TO YOU AS A THANK YOU."

Greg's phone buzzed.

A payment notification.

"$420.69 from GhostDev_69."

Greg's eyes widened. "No freaking way."

CONSIDER IT BUG TESTER'S PAY. NOW DELETE THIS GAME AND NEVER SPEAK OF ME AGAIN.

Greg grinned.

"Nah, man. You're going to make me famous."

The screen flickered one final time.

"I WILL HAUNT YOUR WI-FI FOR ETERNITY."

And then Pixel Paladin IV crashed.

So, if the reader ever boots up a certain cracked version of the game, and knows the right keystrokes mentioned above, you might still hear Eddie whispering through the code.

Mostly swearing about memory leaks.

Whispers

Detective Frank Mulligan of the New South Wales police Northport division didn't believe in ghosts. He barely believed in overtime pay since he seldom saw it. But there he was, standing in the creaky foyer of 113 Maplewood Lane, Northport New South Wales with his notebook in one hand, torch in the other, trying not to let the mildew smell knock him out cold. He read his notes aloud.

"One missing person. Mildred Crenshaw, age 74, last seen watering begonias three days ago. No forced entry, no signs of struggle. Just gone."

He jotted down a few notes.

"Unless she shrank herself down and hid in the vacuum cleaner, she's not here," Frank muttered to himself.

The house didn't argue. It just groaned, as if considering the possibility.

Frank flicked on his torch. The beam cut through the shadows. He'd been in plenty of cases like this before. People don't just vanish without a reason. Most of the time, the reason was buried under a pile of unpaid bills or an empty liquor cabinet. But Mildred's place was tidy. A little too tidy.

As Frank made his way to the kitchen, he heard it.

A whisper.

Soft. Faint.

"In the drawer…"

Frank froze mid-step. His heart, which usually operated at two cups of coffee and mild irritation, picked up speed.

"Hello? Anyone there?"

Silence.

Just the clock ticking above the stove.

He opened the drawer.

Inside was a single pack of gum, wintergreen. He squinted at it like it had insulted him. He pocketed the gum anyway. If the voices were going to give him tips, he might as well stay minty fresh.

He moved to the living room.

The old carpet threatened to eat his shoes whole.

"Do people still have shag carpets?" he thought to himself.

Family photos lined the mantel, smiling faces frozen in time.

That's when he heard it again.

"Behind the book…"

Frank's torch snapped toward the bookshelf.

He shuffled over, finger trailing along the dusty spines. Bird Watching for Beginners. How to Knit a Sweater Your Cat Will Hate. Murder at Maplewood Manor.

"A little on the nose, huh?" he muttered softly.

He tugged on the book. It slid out easily, revealing a small brass key tucked behind it.

Smiling, Frank just said aloud: "Huh… well, now you're just showing off."

Frank pocketed the key while his stomach churned with curiosity and regret. He was wondering if he'd accidentally wandered into a haunted escape room.

Room by room, the whispers led him along.

"In the vase…"

A folded note inside read: Not everything is as it seems.

"Under the rug…"

A loose floorboard, hiding a wad of cash and a receipt for a one-way bus ticket to Perth.

"Check the freezer…"

He found a single frozen meatloaf wrapped in tinfoil.

Finally, the whispers guided him to the bedroom.

The bed was made so tightly. A faint smell of lavender lingered in the air.

"In the closet…"

Frank hesitated. He'd seen enough horror movies to know how this went. But he was too deep now.

He swung open the closet door and found…

A half-knitted sweater.

Cat-sized and it had a small journal tucked inside one sleeve.

Frank flipped it open.

"Dear Diary. If you're reading this, congratulations! You're either a very nosy detective or my nephew, Larry, finally came to check on me. Either way, I've skipped town. Don't worry, I'm not dead, just tired of paying for the neighbour's Amazon packages by accident. That key? It's to the safe deposit box at St George's branch in Northport. The cash was from a bingo night win. And the whispers? That's just my Alexa malfunctioning. Creepy little thing. P.S. The meatloaf's been in the freezer since 2012. Please don't eat it."

Frank closed the journal slowly.

"Well, I'll be damned."

Frank sighs, pulling out the pack of wintergreen gum from his pocket and unwrapping a piece.

"Should've known the only ghost around here was my own common sense."

He chewed thoughtfully, then glanced up at the ceiling.

"Nice touch with the whispers, though."

The house answered with a creak.

Frank froze.

He grabbed his notebook and got the hell out of there.

Three Riders

Joe Caster had seen a lot in his years tending The Cactus Bloom Saloon dust storms that could flay the skin off a cow, bounty hunters who shot first and drank later, even after the time a travelling preacher tried to baptise the whiskey barrel. But he'd never seen a letter like the one that arrived that morning.

The envelope was yellowed and brittle, scrawled in shaky black ink.

"Three riders coming tonight. Harlan Graves, Billy Stokes, and Elvira Kane. All want you dead. Hope you cleaned your pistol."

Joe read the letter twice.

He leaned on the bar, remembering.

Harlan Graves, the outlaw who could hit a rattlesnake's eye from fifty paces. Billy Stokes was a knife fighter, so mean he once stabbed a man for snoring too loud. And Elvira Kane, well, nobody crossed Elvira Kane and lived to talk about it.

Joe sighed.

He poured himself a finger of whiskey.

He hadn't touched a gun in ten years.

The last time he did, he'd put all of them on the ground, or so he'd thought.

"No point hiding the desert don't keep secrets," he muttered.

By sunset, the saloon was empty save for Joe.

He locked the doors and lit the oil lamps.

His old revolver sat heavy on the bar, six bullets in the chamber. He kept glancing at it like it might bite him.

The clock ticked. The wind howled through the cracked boards.

Then the first rider came.

Harlan Graves pushed through the saloon doors, lean and weathered as a dried-out wolf. A scar split his face from brow to chin, the work of Joe's own knife a decade ago.

"Evening, Joe."

Joe poured two glasses of whiskey.

"Evening, Harlan. How's the eye?"

"Still see well enough to shoot."

They drank in silence.

The second rider came an hour later.

Billy Stokes swaggered in, chewing a matchstick. His knife glinted from his belt; the handle worn smooth from a hundred kills.

"Heard there was a funeral happening tonight," Billy says.

Joe didn't pour him whiskey and added: "Help yourself."

"Always liked your hospitality, Joe."

They stood there at the bar, three old enemies waiting for something to break.

Midnight rolled around.

Joe kept his hand near the revolver. His heart pounded like an old drum.

One more rider to come. Elvira Kane.

She rode up as the clock struck twelve.

Her silhouette appeared in the doorway, tall, wrapped in a long red duster. Her silver hair fell loose over her shoulders, one hand resting on the pearl-handled revolver at her hip.

"Well, well," she drawls. "If it ain't Joe Caster. Thought you'd be dead by now."

Joe swallowed hard. "Give it time."

She walked to the bar, boots clicking against the floor. The other two men tensed; hands close to their weapons.

"Reckon you know why we're here, Joe," Elvira says softly.

"Reckon I do."

Harlan leaned forward.

"We all got a bone to pick with you. One night, three graves. Just trying to figure out who gets the first shot."

Joe's fingers brushed the revolver. His mind raced, weighing the odds, counting bullets.

And then he smiled.

It was small at first, a flicker on the corner of his lips. Then it grew wider, slow, and knowing.

Elvira's eyes narrowed. "What's so funny, Joe?"

Joe leaned forward on the bar; his voice was steady. "Y'all ever wonder how three folks I shot dead come riding back into town on the same night?"

The saloon went deathly still.

Harlan's scarred face twitched. Billy shifted in his chair, hand creeping toward his knife. Elvira's hand tightened on her revolver.

Joe's smile never wavered.

"I buried each one of you with my own two hands," he whispered. "Now here you are, clear as day. Either I'm losin' my mind… or something unnatural rode in with the dust tonight."

The wind howled outside. The lamps flickered again.

Harlan's eyes glimmered darkly. Billy's grin faltered. Elvira's fingers trembled in her revolver's grip.

Joe's voice dropped lower.

"How long y'all been riding? Can't remember, can you? How many nights? How many towns?"

No one answered.

The clock struck one.

Joe slowly reached beneath the bar for the half-empty bottle of whiskey. He poured three glasses.

"Might as well have a drink," he said. "Before the sun comes up. Before you figure out what you really are."

The riders stared at him, uncertain now. The wind outside kicked harder, rattling the windows.

Billy's hand fell away from his knife. Harlan's scarred face slackened. Elvira's breath caught in her throat.

They all drank.

By dawn, the glasses were empty.

Joe stood alone at the bar, watching the sun creep over the desert.

The three riders were gone.

There were no bodies. There were no tracks.

Just dust and whispers.

He poured himself one last drink, hands steady now.

"I told myself the desert don't keep secrets," he muttered.

The whiskey burned down his throat, hot and smooth.

Outside, the wind carried three names away into the rising light.

Names long buried.

Names that were never meant to rise again.

My Ultimate Wisdom

Clara Montgomery had spent her whole life trying to live up to the wisdom of her father, Dr Harold Montgomery, the world's most beloved self-help guru.

His book Unlock Your Inner Magnificence had sold hundred and forty million copies worldwide in several languages and inspired everything from yoga retreats to scented candle lines.

If someone wanted to live their best life, they'd probably read Harold's words while balancing crystals on their forehead.

When Harold passed away at the ripe old age of ninety-one, the world mourned.

Clara, meanwhile, found herself buried under mountains of fan letters, inspirational calendars, and scented soy candles that all smelled suspiciously like sandalwood and unresolved childhood trauma.

But the genuine treasure lay in the back of his office closet, an unpublished manuscript sealed in a battered manila envelope, scrawled with the words: My Ultimate Wisdom.

Clara poured herself a glass of merlot and sat down at the desk where her father had written his bestsellers. She took a deep breath, opened the envelope, and read the first chapter titled: The Voice of Enlightenment.

"For years, people have asked me where I discovered my profound insights. The answer, dear reader, is Wilbur."

Clara blinked and took another sip of wine.

Wilbur?

"Wilbur, my African Grey parrot, came into my life during a particularly challenging time shortly after my divorce from Barbara and during an unfortunate experiment with kale smoothies. He began speaking to me late at night, offering guidance in matters both spiritual and practical."

Clara set the glass down slowly.

Her father, the man who once advised celebrities and heads of state in gratitude journals, had been taking career advice from a bird?

"Wilbur's first teaching came on a stormy night in 1983. I had just burned a batch of lentil loaf when he said, quite clearly, 'Let it go.' At first, I thought I was hallucinating from the smell of charred legumes. But Wilbur repeated it three times. 'Let it go. Let it go. LET IT GO.' I knew then that I had heard the voice of wisdom."

Clara slapped the manuscript shut and stared at the ceiling.

The entire Forgiveness Is Your Superpower chapter from his third book had been inspired by a bird telling him to forget about burnt lentils.

She flipped to the next page where she read chapter two: Feathered Affirmations

"Wilbur's teachings were often concise, yet profound. His most famous lesson 'You are enough' was delivered while he was staring at himself in a compact mirror. He repeated it every morning. Sometimes with minor variations, like 'You're the best, Wilbur' or 'Who's a handsome boy?' But the meaning was always clear."

Clara's mouth hung open.

The mantra that had fuelled thousands of guided hundreds of thousands of meditations printed on decorative pillows and tattooed on at least four of her ex-boyfriends had been ripped directly from a narcissistic parrot.

By the time Clara got to chapter six Seed Diets and the Art of Mindful Snacking, Clara was halfway through the bottle of merlot.

"He never shut up," she muttered aloud. "I thought Dad kept him around for company, not because he was the bird-brained Buddha."

She glanced at the ancient birdcage still sitting in the office's corner, still there after Wilbur had passed on years ago.

Clara continued reading. Chapter nine: The Breakthrough.

"One night, Wilbur gave me the secret to happiness. It was so profound; I nearly dropped my cup of chamomile tea. He said... 'Don't poop where you sleep.'"

Clara choked on her wine.

"That's not life advice, Dad! That's basic hygiene!"

By dawn, she'd finished the manuscript.

It was nearly four hundred pages of recycled self-help jargon, interspersed with the ramblings of a bird with a god complex. The whole self-help empire had been built on the existential musings of a feathered narcissist.

Clara had two choices:

Burn the manuscript and take the secret to her grave.

Publish it and let the world know that the greatest self-help spiritual teacher ever born had spent most of his career nodding along to bird babble.

Her phone buzzed with a text from her father's publisher.

"Hey Clara! Hope you're holding up okay. Any chance that the final manuscript is ready? Can't wait to get your father's last masterpiece out into the world."

Clara stared at the screen.

Her father's face beamed from every inspirational coffee mug and podcast thumbnail.

"People needed guidance. People needed hope," Clara said aloud.

What people did not need to know was that they'd been quoting an African Grey parrot who used to scream "CLEAN YOUR FEATHERS" during every dinner.

She sighed and opened her laptop.

One month later, the book hit the shelves under the title My Ultimate Wisdom: Wisdom from a Lifetime of Listening.

Critics called it a groundbreaking exploration of interspecies enlightenment.

Several talk show hosts added it to their book club, which meant that over one million books sold the first month to club members alone.

None other than Percy Nightingale, who made the line "Polly wants inner peace" sound so profound that the audiobook sold over five hundred thousand copies alone.

Clara told no one the truth.

But now and then, when she stood in the self-help aisle of the bookstore, she'd swears she heard her father's voice in a faint whisper from somewhere far away saying: "Who's a wise boy? You are Wilbur. You are…"

CURRICULUM VITAE

After for four hundred and seventy-six years of loyal service, Merlinus the Wizard had had enough.

He slammed the castle door behind him, letting the echo rattle through the stone halls. His beard was a majestic white cascade that could have doubled as a small tapestry swayed indignantly as he marched toward the Royal Library.

"Four centuries of fireballs, prophecies, and enchanted chamber pots and for what?" he muttered. "To be asked to conjure a birthday cake for the royal corgi? I didn't study under the Archimage of Eternal Mysteries to become a glorified baker!"

He flung open the heavy oak door of the library and snatched a parchment from the nearest desk. He wrote his curriculum vitae and to give it to the queen so she could have reference to hire her next wizard. He sat down and scratched furiously across the page.

Curriculum Vitae — Wizard Position (Reluctantly Vacated)

Name: Merlinus the Wizard, B.A. (Bachelor of Alchemy), M.P.M. (Master of Potion Mismanagement), Grand High Order of the Pointy Hat Society

Objective: To finally retire in peace without being summoned at odd hours to uncurse the Queen's hairpins or retrieve Sir Percival from the moat.

Experience:

476 years as Royal Wizard to Her Majesty Queen Lavinia the Persistent

Successfully prevented seventeen apocalypses (though two were self-inflicted because of unauthorised spell experimentation).

Transformed a goose into a prince, however, regrettably, the prince maintained certain… honking tendencies.

Brewed the Elixir of Eternal Youth but the results are inconclusive since the Queen insists, she still feels fifty-seven.

Summoned exactly one demon, accidentally, during the Great Pudding Incident of 1433.

Regularly advised on matters of state, astrology, and which curtains would best match the royal throne room.

Skills:

Advanced spell casting in Fireball, Lightning Bolt, Making It Look Like You Know What You're Doing flashes.

Potion brewing.

Diplomacy with talking frogs.

Fluent in five dead languages.

Uncursing objects that should never have been cursed in the first place.

References:

Sir Percival, who I might add, is still partially amphibious.

The Enchanted Mirror.

Gerald the Gargoyle.

Salary Expectations: One tower. No corgis.

Satisfied, he rolled up the parchment and stomped toward the Queen's throne room. He burst through the gilded doors, ignoring the startled yelps of courtiers.

Queen Lavinia, in her usual state of regal obliviousness, barely looked up from her embroidery.

"Ah, Merlinus. Did you bring the corgi cake?"

"I am retiring, Your Majesty!" he declares, flinging the parchment onto her lap.

The Queen arched an eyebrow. "Again?"

"This time it's final. I am done with your corgis, your enchanted hairpins, and Sir Percival's amphibious misadventures."

She picked up the scroll, her eyes scanning the contents.

"Uncursing chamber pots… preventing apocalypses… Advanced spell casting… Whistled language?"

"It's quite popular in the underworld," Merlinus sniffed.

The Queen nodded thoughtfully. "And the goose prince?"

"Still honking."

She leaned back, twirling a needle between her fingers. "Very well, Merlinus. If you're certain…"

"Absolutely."

"And you'll be leaving behind all your spell books?"

Merlinus's eye twitched. He hadn't considered that.

"A wizard must travel light," he muttered.

"And your self-replenishing wine goblet?"

Merlinus's lips pursed. He had very much considered that.

The Queen smiled sweetly. "Well then, I shall miss you terribly. I hope the new wizard will be half as competent."

Merlinus snatched the parchment back.

"On second thought," he grumbled, "I'll stay until you find someone who can tell the difference between a sleeping draught and a love potion."

The Queen beamed. "I knew you'd come around. Now, be a dear and conjure me up a corgi cake."

My Guy**

Myrtle Pinkerton was not the kind of woman you'd expect to start a scandal in the sleepy town of Northport, New South Wales.

At 72 years young, she was best known for running the church bake sale, aggressively feeding the neighbourhood cats, and wearing cardigans that seemed to multiply in pastel colours every season.

But if there was one thing Myrtle took more seriously than her prize-winning lemon drizzle cake, it was her devotion to one man: Franklin P. Pinkerton.

"My guy," she called him.

Franklin, with his mismatched socks, receding hairline, and an unhealthy fondness for vegemite and pickle sandwiches, was not what you'd call a heartthrob.

But to Myrtle, he was the cream of the crop.

The Top of the Pops.

And the butter to her biscuits.

"He may not be a movie star," she tells anyone who would listen, usually the cashier at the grocery store or Mrs Haggerty at the bingo hall, "but when it comes to being happy, we are."

Northport had seen its fair share of gossip, but nothing quite like the unwavering loyalty of Myrtle Pinkerton.

It all started one fateful Tuesday when a new fitness instructor named Dirk Thunderstorm (yes, that was his real name) set up a Zumba class at the community centre. Dirk was the kind of man whose biceps had biceps. His smile could melt butter at thirty paces, and his cologne smelled like a cross between pine trees and an ATO tax refund.

Women flocked to him like seagulls to a chip van.

All the women, except Myrtle Pinkerton.

"Oh no," she says firmly, as Mrs Haggerty elbowed her to join the Zumba line. "No muscle-bound man could take me away from my guy."

Dirk Thunderstorm, who had never been turned down by anyone over the age of sixty, took this as a challenge.

"Myrtle," he purrs, flexing his triceps. "What if I could teach you to salsa like you're twenty-five again?"

"I gave my guy my word of honour," she declared, adjusting her knitted hat. "To be faithful, and I'm going to."

Dirk Thunderstorm blinked.

No one.

NO ONE resisted Dirk Thunderstorm.

He tossed in a free smoothie coupon and a wink.

Myrtle took the coupon, stuffed it in her handbag, and walked straight out of that community centre like a woman on a mission.

Word spread like wildfire.

Myrtle Pinkerton had turned down Dirk Thunderstorm.

The other ladies whispered behind their bingo cards. Mrs Haggerty practically needed smelling salts. Even Reverend Middlestone paused during his sermon to give Myrtle an approving nod.

But Dirk was not done.

Oh no. The man might have muscles that lasted for days, but his pride was twice as big.

The next morning, a bouquet of roses arrived at Myrtle's door.

"From Dirk," the delivery boy says with a wink.

"Nothing you could buy could make me tell a lie to my guy," Myrtle mutters, slamming the door.

By Thursday, the whole town was in a frenzy.

Dirk had offered Myrtle a free gym membership, a custom protein shake called "Thunder Berry Blitz," and a lifetime supply of lavender-scented muscle rub. Myrtle turned it all down without so much as batting an eyelash.

One day Mary Sullivan overheard Myrtle saying: "You know, Mrs Haggerty, I think my Franklin is the tops. He's the cream of the crop." She tells Mrs Haggerty as they walked home from the post office, arm in arm.

But by Friday, things had taken a turn.

Dirk Thunderstorm was not used to losing.

He resorted to desperate measures, plastering Myrtle's front lawn with posters of his shirtless Zumba poses. He even tried serenading her with a portable karaoke machine in the dead of night. Myrtle simply pulled the curtains, sipped her chamomile tea, and turned up the volume on her knitting podcast.

Northport was divided.

Half the town wanted Myrtle to cave in, if only for the spectacle of watching her salsa across the community centre floor. The other half began wearing "Team Myrtle" badges and started writing strongly worded letters to Dirk Thunderstorm's fitness newsletter.

Finally, on Saturday morning, Dirk showed up at Myrtle's door holding a single sunflower and looking thoroughly defeated.

"Myrtle," he sighs. "I admit defeat. You're the only woman in Northport who's immune to my charms. What's your secret?"

Myrtle peered at him over her half-moon glasses.

"Dirk," she says softly, "when you've found your guy, no handsome face could ever take the place of him."

Franklin P. Pinkerton, who had been napping in his armchair, snorted awake just in time to hear this. He blinked, looked around, and promptly fell back asleep, drooling slightly.

Dirk Thunderstorm trudged back to the community centre, defeated.

And Myrtle?

Myrtle simply tucked the sunflower into a vase, brewed another pot of tea, and went back to knitting Franklin a cardigan that would clash horribly with the six others he already owned.

Because when it came to being happy, they were.

As a matter of fact.

**With my deep apologies to Ms Mary Wells, singer and performer and Mr William Robinson Jr songwriter.

Aunt Beatrix Vintage Emporium

If there was one place in the small town of Northport, New South Wales that always smelled like equal parts mothballs, Vaseline petroleum mixed with a lavender air freshener, it was Aunt Beatrix's Vintage Emporium. Nestled between a failing juice bar and an eyebrow threading studio, the shop hadn't seen a customer under the age of seventy since disco was in style.

That is until Zoe Thompson and Dylan McIntyre got summer jobs there.

Zoe applied because she needed cash for concert tickets.

Dylan applied because his mom says he needed to build "character." Neither of them knew how to fold clothes properly, but both were convinced the other would get fired first.

"Ten bucks says I outlast you," Zoe declares on their first day, balancing a mannequin head on one hip.

"Deal," Dylan shot back.

After a few weeks, Miss Beatrix Fermin trusted them enough to let them run the store by themselves. At seventy-one years of age, she would open the store and leave around lunchtime to go home and watch the afternoon soap operas, especially "Home and Away" leaving them to close shop, and both Zoe and Dylan rose up to the challenge.

"How hard could it be to run the store ourselves?" they both say. But the one thing they did not expect was Aunt Beatrix's Vintage Emporium's clothes.

It started with a maroon leather jacket from the 1980s that smelled like stale cigarettes.

"Check this out," Dylan says, sliding it on. "I feel like I should be in a band called The Misunderstood Mustaches."

Before Zoe could roll her eyes, Dylan froze.

His eyes glazed over, and his mouth opened slightly.

"Marsha, I told you the microwave is NOT for drying socks!" he mumbles in a voice that did not sound like his own.

"What the hell, Dylan?"

Dylan blinked and ripped the jacket off like it was on fire.

"What? What just happened?"

Zoe snatched the jacket, holding it at arm's length like it might bite. "You blacked out and started yelling at someone named Marsha."

"Oh god. What if a dead guy who lived in his mom's basement possessed me or something?"

"Or what if these clothes show the memories of the people who donated them?" Zoe adds.

They stared at each other.

"Only one way to find out," Zoe says and grabbed a leopard print scarf off the rack and wrapped it around her neck.

A second later, she was singing the Macarena in flawless Spanish.

By the end of their shift, the duo confirmed two things:

First, the clothes showed memories of the person who owned them and second, most people in Northport had really boring lives.

It became a game.

Each night after closing, Zoe and Dylan volunteer to stay back and clean up and straighten the store, and after they did, they try on the weirdest stuff they could find.

Dylan put on a polyester tracksuit and ran laps around the shop, swearing in Russian.

Zoe tried on a feather boa and belted out three verses of I Will Survive in a whiskey-soaked baritone.

They were having the best summer of their lives.

Until they accidentally found their own parents' clothes.

Zoe was sorting through a bag of donations when she pulled out a neon green tank top that looked suspiciously familiar.

"No way…" she whispered, turning it inside out.

Sure enough, written on the tag in Sharpie: Property of Kim T.

"Kim T." was her mom, aka the reigning champion of passive-aggressive guilt trips.

"Put it on," Dylan grinned.

"Absolutely not."

"Come on," he teases. "What's the worst that could happen? You learn she was cool once?"

Zoe glared but tugged the shirt over her head.

Immediately, she was transported to 1994.

Kim Thompson, her mother, was crowd-surfing at a Pearl Jam concert, screaming, "I LOVE YOU, EDDIE VEDDER!" with two beers in one hand and a guy named Trevor braiding her hair.

When Zoe snapped out of it, she was hyperventilating.

"My mother was fun?"

"It seems, Zoe, that your mom was a total groupie." Dylan says.

Zoe ripped the shirt off and stuffed it in the back of a drawer where it would never see the light of day again.

"Your turn, Dylan."

Zoe went to the men's section, grabbed a navy-blue jacket, and held it out.

"No way. Look at the name on the back." Dylan says.

The name stitched on the back: McIntyre.

"Do it," Zoe says.

Dylan slipped the jacket on.
His eyes glazed over.

"Coach said… if I score one more touchdown… I can have the Camaro… but I don't need the Camaro… because I have the prettiest girl at Northport High."

Zoe's jaw dropped. "YOUR DAD WAS A PLAYER?!"

Dylan ripped the jacket off like it was on fire.

"Nope. No way. That never happened."

"Oh, it happened." Zoe grinned.

By the end of the summer, the store was their secret kingdom, a place where polyester and corduroy whispered stories of forgotten lives.

They made a pact:

One memory a night and tell no one what they saw.

Well, except for Mrs Carter's hot-air balloon proposal in 1978, because that was just too good not to share.

On their last shift, they stood in front of the locked door, the neon CLOSE sign flickering behind them.

"So, what happens to the memories now?" Dylan asks.

"No idea. Maybe they fade. Maybe they wait for someone else to find them."

They glanced at the racks of clothes.

Aunt Beatrix's Vintage Emporium would always be full of secrets stitched into seams, hidden in hems, and whispered through forgotten pockets.

As they walked away into the warm night, Dylan slung an arm around Zoe's shoulder.

"Ten bucks says I outlasted you next summer."

Zoe grinned.

"Double or nothing."

As Zoe and Dylan walked away, the clothes in the window rustled ever so slightly behind them.

Waiting for their return.

Crimes Against Matrimony

It was a dark and stormy Tuesday evening, or at least it felt like it was in Brenda's heart. The clock ticked on the wall, each second hammering her patience thinner and thinner. Her husband, Gary, was late. Again. Not that she kept a ledger of his tardiness okay, she absolutely did, with dates, times, and little angry frowny faces in the margins of her secret notebook labelled Gary's Crimes Against Matrimony.

Brenda had simmered in silent fury for the better part of an hour. The leftover lasagna was cold, the wine bottle half-empty (because she had poured herself a "calm down" glass… or three), and the dog, Mr. Pickles, had long since abandoned her for the couch.

Finally, an idea sparked. Enough was enough.

She scribbled a note with the fury of a woman pushed too far:

"I've had enough. I've left you. Don't bother coming after me."

She paused dramatically before adding a small flourish under the word enough, just in case Gary missed the emotional weight of the whole situation.

With the note placed strategically on his pillow, she crouched down and wiggled under the bed like a ninja fuelled entirely by Pinot Grigio and spite. Her heart pounded as she tucked herself in, determined to see how much her absence would devastate him.

Minutes passed.

Then the front door creaked open.

Keys jingled. Shoes shuffled.

Gary whistled.

He's whistling? WHISTLING? Brenda's blood pressure spiked.

She heard him clatter around the kitchen, probably snacking on the garlic bread she deliberately didn't warm up. He was the type to eat cold leftovers without a single complaint, and that alone infuriated her more.

Finally, he wandered into the bedroom.

Through the narrow gap between the dust bunnies, Brenda watched him approach the dresser. He spotted the note, picked it up… and just stood there.

The room filled with an agonizing silence. This was it. He was reading her farewell. He was breaking inside.

Any second now, she expected to hear the guttural wail of a man, realizing he had taken his one true love for granted.

Instead, there was a faint scratching sound. A pen. He was writing something.

Brenda's breath caught in her throat. A love letter? A desperate plea for forgiveness?

Then he pulled out his phone.

"Hey babe, she's finally gone."

Brenda's heart slammed into her ribcage.

"Yeah, I know about bloody time."

Her whole body stiffened, limbs going numb. WHO WAS HE TALKING TO?

"I'm coming to see you, so put on that sexy French nightie."

Her whole life flashed before her eyes: her the wedding, the mortgage, the time she let him name the dog Mr. Pickles even though she wanted to call him Fluffy. It had all been a lie.

"I love you and I can't wait to see you. We'll do all the naughty things you like."

Gary chuckles, low and dirty, and hung up the phone.

Brenda's hands balled into fists under the bed.

She was already composing a list of possible murder weapons in her head. The rolling pin, the decorative samurai sword Gary insists, was "just for display," or perhaps death by lasagna poisoning.

Finally, she heard the front door shut and the car engine rev to life.

The betrayal.

The audacity.

The waiting.

Crawling out from under the bed like a woman possessed, Brenda snatched the note off the pillow. Her eyes darted down to where Gary had scrawled beneath her dramatic message:

"I can see your feet under the bed. We're out of bread. I will be back in five minutes."

Brenda blinked.

She stared at the note, went downstairs, and poured herself another glass of wine.

Gary came home seventeen minutes later.

He brought home a six-pack of his favourite beer: Great Northern Super Crisp, but no bread.

But there was a suspiciously warm garlic bread waiting for him in the oven.

And Brenda slept like a baby that night.

Time And Love

Dr Malcolm Green never meant to invent a time machine. He was supposed to be perfecting a self-heating coffee mug. But somewhere between adjusting the thermoregulator and a rogue particle accelerator experiment, he accidentally opened a rift in the space-time continuum. It happens, you know.

He only realised what he'd done when he pressed the button marked "Reheat" and found himself in the middle of a medieval market square, clutching his half-drunk coffee while a man in a tunic offered to trade him two goats for it.

Once Malcolm managed to bumble his way back to his lab, an ordeal involving a chicken, a trebuchet, and a very confused knight, he locked the machine up, swore to dismantle it, and vowed to stick to coffee-related pursuits.

Then he saw her.

Amidst the bustling medieval market, she moved with quiet confidence, her copper-red hair cascading in loose waves past her shoulders, catching the sunlight like molten bronze. Her high cheekbones were dusted with freckles that danced across her fair skin, testimony to days spent outdoors despite nobility's preference for alabaster paleness.

Her eyes, the clear green of spring leaves, surveyed the market stalls with intelligent curiosity. She wore a forest-green kirtle that complemented her colouring, the fabric finer than most, with sleeves that tapered elegantly at her wrists.

She bumped into him. Stopped and gave him a smile and all the suddenly she leaned and gave him a kiss. Malcom disappeared in a flash of blue light.

The next thing Malcom knows is that he is in a 1920s Speakeasy right in the middle of a smoky basement bar filled with flapper dresses and jazz. He stumbled into a wooden booth, adjusting his thick glasses, still clutching his ever-present coffee mug.

"Rough night, professor?"

Malcolm looked up. This time she had red lipstick, her hair still fiery red but with curls, and that same smile that could knock him out.

"Hi, yes. I'm Dr Malcolm Green. I did not introduce myself last time. Had no time…"

"Veronica." She offered her hand, and when he shook it.

They talked for an hour.

She was funny, sharp, and kept calling him "Doc" like she was in some old movie. He was just wondering if maybe time travel wasn't the worst thing when she leaned in and kissed him.

And Malcolm promptly vanished in a flash of blue light.

The third time Malcolm saw her, he was halfway through being accused of witchcraft by a band of very large, very bearded Norsemen. She walked out of a longhouse, wrapped in furs, the same dark curls falling around her face.

"Oh, for Odin's sake," she sighed. "What is it this time?"

Malcolm's mouth opened and closed. "You know me?"

"You show up in the weirdest places, Doc."

Veronica smuggled him out of the village, and they spent the night watching the aurora borealis dance across the sky. This time, she kissed him by a crackling fire.

Blue flash. Gone again.

Malcolm materialised inside a glass-domed city on Mars.

According to the large electronic timer on the wall, the time was Mars time: 14:23, year 3233, location Mars Space Colony 2147.

Malcolm waked over to a vending machine that sold nutrient paste in three exciting flavours.

"Coffee, black. Please?" he muttered out of habit.

"It's still disgusting," said a familiar voice.

He whirled around. Veronica wore a sleek silver jumpsuit, her curls tucked into a high ponytail. She looked the same; timeless, literally.

"How? How do you keep finding me?"

"I'm not finding you. You're finding me."

They sat in a booth overlooking the red sands. The sky was full of stars, and Malcolm told her everything. The machine, the accidents, how he was quite sure he was breaking several laws of physics just by existing.

She listened like she'd heard it before. Maybe she had.

They kissed under the Martian sky. And he vanished.

Malcolm barely had time to adjust to the smell of salt and gunpowder before someone shoved a sword into his hand and called him a filthy landlubber.

Veronica was standing at the ship's helm, wearing a tricorn hat, and grinning like she'd been born to plunder.

"I was wondering when you'd show up," she said.

They spent three days avoiding mutiny, playing cards, and stealing rum. When she finally kissed him on the deck under the moonlight, Malcolm barely had time to groan, "Not again," before the blue light swallowed him up.

Malcolm blinked and found himself back in his lab. The coffee mug still sat half-empty on his workbench. The machine whirred softly. Had it all been a dream?

Then there was a knock on the door.

He opened it, heart pounding.

Veronica stood there, in jeans and a leather jacket, holding two paper cups from the coffee shop down the street.

"Thought you could use a refill, Doc."

Malcolm gaped. "You are here? How?"

"I figured you out a long time ago." She smirked. "Took you long enough to catch up."

He could barely breathe as she stepped inside. He tried to think of something smart, to say something scientific, maybe, but then she kissed him.

No blue flash.

Just the sound of the machine powering down, and the slow realisation that he was exactly where he was supposed to be.

"Finally," Veronica murmurs in his ears.

Malcolm grinned. He did not know how long he'd been chasing her or how long she'd been waiting for him.

But as he set down his coffee mug and tangled his fingers in her curls, he knew one thing for certain:

Some things, like time and love, are best left unsolved.

Secrets

The rain drummed softly against the windows of the Northport Public Library, casting a rhythm over the nearly deserted building. Oliver Kane, the library's head librarian, sat behind the worn oak circulation desk, cataloguing a recent donation of old books. He was a man of quiet habits, with round glasses perched on his nose and a penchant for solving crossword puzzles on his lunch break.

It was just after closing when Oliver's fingers brushed across the spine of a battered leather-bound book titled Tales of the Southern Cross. The cover was faded, its corners dog-eared. It had been tucked away at the bottom of a box, forgotten.

With a sigh, Oliver opened the book.

As he turned the brittle pages, something crinkled beneath his fingertips. Tucked between the yellowed sheets was a folded sheet of paper, edges browned with age.

His curiosity piqued; and Oliver unfolded the note.

Scrawled in careful, looping handwriting was a series of letters and numbers: G43 – W17 – T29 – S8.

A code.

Oliver's mind immediately went into overdrive with ideas.

He recognised the style. It was a cipher often used in the early 20th century to indicate book locations. But why hide such a code in an old book? It was late, and he needed to close the library for the night. "I'll look at it in the morning," he muttered to no one as he packed his desk, and closed the old doors to the library and locked them for the evening.

The following morning, Oliver set to work.

The library's archives dated back nearly a century, and the numbered sections matched the original cataloguing system from the 1950s. He traced the first coordinate, G43, to a shelf in the back corner of the archives, where dust clung to forgotten novels. There, tucked between two volumes on local flora, he found another note.

This one is more explicit.

"Northport. 1954. She never came home," it read.

Oliver felt an odd chill as he ventured into the old microfiche newspaper's storage area where he found a table and started his research as he tapped his fingers nervously as he scanned the headlines. Then he found it a small article buried in the back pages of the Northport Gazette.

Missing: Eleanor Bright, age 23. Last seen leaving the Northport train station on June 14, 1954.

The case had never been solved.

The brief article noted Eleanor was a secretary at the old Northport Mill.

There were no suspects.

No leads.

Just another name lost to time.

Oliver quickly started looking up the remaining coordinates, each leading to another clue hidden in long-forgotten books.

A pressed flower inside a poetry collection.

A ticket stub from the Northport Theatre.

A locket with the initials E.B. etched inside.

Someone had been leaving breadcrumbs for decades, a trail meant to be followed.

By the time Oliver reached the final coordinate, dusk again was settling over Northport. He needed to hurry. He had left Mildred Feinstein all along to handle the library's customers, and she must be wondering what he had been up to.

He now stood in the library's attic when he noticed something hidden behind a loose brick in the wall.

It was the last note, written in the same delicate handwriting:

"He waits where the tide breaks."

The beach.

The next morning, Oliver called in sick, his first sick day in three years, and followed the note's cryptic direction to the rocky shoreline at the edge of town. The tide was low, revealing jagged rocks and hidden crevices. After an hour of searching, he found it a rusted lockbox wedged deep inside a hollowed-out rock.

Inside the box was a stack of letters, all signed with the initials H.W.

Bingo thought Oliver.

This is the same Harold Whitman, the foreman at the Northport Mill, according to his memory of reading all the microfiche newspapers.

The letters spoke of forbidden meetings and whispered promises. Harold had been in love with Eleanor Bright, but the last letter was darker.

It hinted at jealousy of a confrontation of a secret that needed burying.

Oliver's heart ached as he pieced the story together.

Harold must have hidden the letters out of guilt, scattering clues across the library where Eleanor once spent her lunch breaks. Perhaps he had hoped someone would uncover the truth, but no one ever did.

Until now.

Oliver returned the letters to the police, who reopened the case.

The revelations sent ripples through Northport, drawing out whispers of long-buried secrets.

Though the crime would never be fully solved, Eleanor's name finally found its way back into the light, thanks to Oliver Kane.

As for Oliver Kane, he returned to his quiet life among the books.

But sometimes, when the rain tapped against the windows and the library grew still, he would run his fingers over the spines of the oldest volumes, listening for the whispers buried in the stacks.

Waiting for the next secret to reveal itself.

The Riddles Of Ophir

In the dim glow of a lantern, Clara Hartwell read the last lines of her uncle's will. The words chilled her more than the winter wind rattling the panes of the old ranch house.

"The cattle are yours, Clara, as is the land. But there is another inheritance, hidden beneath the hills. Solve the riddles, and the gold of Toothless Edward Harkins shall be yours."

Clara folded the parchment and her heart quickening.

She'd heard the stories whispered in the taverns of Orange, New South Wales, about the prospector who disappeared in 1838 with a fortune in gold. Some claimed he had died in the hills, others that he'd buried the treasure so deep no man could ever claim it.

No man, perhaps, but how about a woman?

It was getting late, so Clara waited till morning to research what her uncle had said in the will.

The next morning, Clara searched her uncle's cluttered study. Tucked inside a battered ledger, she found a slip of yellowed paper.

"Where the waterfalls, the moon will rise, a hollow marked by sunken eyes."

She knew the land well enough. Just beyond the cattle pens, Ophir Creek wound through a narrow gorge. Clara saddled her mare and rode along the bank until she reached the waterfall.

"What am I supposed to look for, Uncle?" she says to herself.

The sun had nearly set when she spotted them.

Two small caves carved into the limestone. She dismounted and stepped inside the cave on the right.

With the sunlight almost gone, she saw nothing and quickly came out of the cave and headed into the cave on the left.

After walking in for a few metres, she spotted it.

It was a rusted tin box lay half-buried beneath a cairn of stones. Inside was another slip of paper.

"By blade of thorn where widows cry, beneath the branches shadows lie."

"The old blackthorn tree," Clara thought.

The night settled thick and cold over the hills. Her uncle's grave stood behind the house, beneath a twisted blackthorn tree. The branches creaked in the wind, making them sound like bones shifting in the dark.

Clara took a spade from her barn and dug at the base of the tree. The earth was loose, as if disturbed before. Her spade struck something hard; a small wooden box wrapped in oilcloth.

Inside was another note.

"Where the sun sinks, the serpent coils. Beneath the stone, the fortune toils."

Clara almost shouted.

She knew the place. It was called Serpent's Bend, where the creek curved like a snake beneath the western hills.

Clara waited until dawn before setting out.

The bend lay half a day's ride from the ranch. As she approached, the sky darkened, heavy with rain. The hills whispered as the wind swept through the grass.

She searched for hours, fingers raw from turning over stones. The rain fell, soaking her dress, washing mud down the slopes.

Finally, beneath a flat slab near the creek's edge, her spade struck wood.

A small chest, bound in iron.

Clara pried it open. The gold gleamed even beneath the grey sky.

Coins, nuggets, and rough ingots piled high. The stolen fortune of Toothless Edward Harkins.

A chill wrapped around her, colder than the rain. For a moment, she thought she heard laughter echoing through the trees high and rasping, like a man who had long forgotten how to smile.

Clara brought the chest back to her ranch and buried it beneath the floorboards of the ranch house, sealing the gold away. She tended her uncle's cattle, worked the land, and never spoke of what she had found.

She would share this one day with the right man.

A man, who would walk into her life, see her all alone struggling with the land and with no hesitation would jump in to help.

But until said man walked into her life, she would sit in her ranch house and listen to what seemed like footsteps pacing beneath the floor and a voice, low and toothless, whispering riddles in the dark.

Two Left Feet

Charlene Preston had precisely two reasons for joining the Tuesday evening salsa class at Rhythm & Brews Dance Studio: First to improve coordination before she accidentally walked into another glass door at work and second to get out of the house before she started naming the houseplants again. Charlene had gotten way too confident with Fernando the fern.

What Charlene did not expect was to come face-to-face with the reason they avoided going out in public in the first place: Leo Martinez her high school heartthrob with a smile of a Greek god, and the reason Charlene once walked straight into a vending machine in tenth grade.

Charlene froze in the doorway, one sneaker half-on and already sweating through her t-shirt.

Leo stood at the front of the room, demonstrating a basic step with the kind of effortless confidence that should've been illegal. His hair was still perfect. His smile was still stupid. And his hips, dear sweet gravity, his hips could file for copyright infringement.

"Welcome, everyone! I'm Leo, and I'll be your instructor."

Charlene felt her soul leave her body.

"This is a beginner class," Leo continued, completely unaware that his presence had just turned one clumsy 30-year-old into a human-shaped puddle. "No pressure, no judgment. Just fun."

Charlene attempted to casually back out of the room like a spy in an awful movie, only to trip over a stack of yoga mats and land directly on their own butt. The entire class turned.

Leo's smile flicked toward them. Oh no. He had dimples. When did he get dimples?

"You okay back there?" Leo asked, eyes twinkling.

Charlene scrambled up so fast she almost took down a coat rack. "Totally fine! Just testing the gravity in this room. Seems very present."

Smooth. Very smooth.

The class paired off to practice basic steps. Charlene ended up with a man named Lando, who had the patience of a saint and the grip strength of a professional wrestler.

"Left foot forward, right foot back," Leo called out, weaving through the couples. "Don't overthink it. Just let your body follow the music."

Charlene's body, unfortunately, preferred following the music like a toddler trying to parallel park.

"Relax your shoulders," Leo said, suddenly appearing right beside her. His hand rested lightly on Charlene's arm.

Charlene's brain blue screened.

"Breathe in," Leo instructed. "One… two… three—"

Charlene exhaled directly into Leo's face. It smelled like a full gust of stale coffee breath.

Leo blinked, but somehow, he did not recoil.

Either he was incredibly professional or had lost all sense of smell.

By the time the class ended, Charlene had stepped on three people's feet, accidentally hip-checked Lando into the water cooler, and learned approximately zero actual dance moves. They were halfway out the door when Leo called out.

"Hey, Charlene?"

Charlene froze.

"How did he…? Oh no. Of course. He knew her," she thought to herself.

"You know, Charlene, your dancing's not that bad."

"Are you lying to me right now?"

Leo grinned. Dimples. Again, with those damn dimples.

"Maybe a little. But if you're planning on sticking around, I could give you some one-on-one lessons."

Charlene's brain screamed, "RED ALERT! FLIRTING DETECTED!" while her mouth betrayed her entirely by saying: "Sure! Yeah! Totally! Unless you want to preserve your toes. I hear they're important for dancing."

Leo had an actual, honest-to-goodness chuckle, and Charlene suddenly didn't care how many vending machines they'd walked into in this lifetime.

Maybe having two left feet was not the worst thing in the world, especially if they led you right back to someone, you'd never quite forgotten.

Talking Machines

Cooper Branson wasn't exactly the best scavenger in the wasteland. He wasn't even in the top fifty. His reputation floated somewhere between "guy who once traded half a can of peaches for a broken toaster" and "that idiot who got his foot stuck in a tire for two days."

He preferred the term "survivor."

The thing about surviving in the end times was that most people were hunting for food, water, or weapons. Cooper? He had a very different priority: cool stuff.

He liked junk.

Weird, shiny, old-world junk.

Pocket watches that didn't tick.

Melted plastic action figures.

Once, he found an entire vending machine keypad and carried it around for three months because pressing the buttons made him feel important.

So, when Cooper stumbled into a half-buried electronics store on the outskirts of Northport in New South Wales, he wasn't looking for anything practical. He was looking for treasures.

That's when he found the radio.

It sat on a shelf behind some water-damaged TVs, half-covered in dust and what Cooper liked to call "wasteland seasoning." It was one of those chunky old machines with knobs the size of baby fists and an antenna bent like it owed someone money.

He poked at it.

Nothing.

He poked at it harder, and it crackled to life.

A voice, faint and crackly, whispered through the static,

"Mayday… anyone out there… please… need help… coordinates… 23.105, -109.432… repeat… Mayday."

Cooper stared at the radio like it had insulted his mother.

"Aw, hell no."

Talking machines were never a good sign.

Last time he found one, it was a busted AI refrigerator that kept calling him "Karen" and demanding to know if he wanted crushed ice.

He leaned in, eyes squinting at the dials.

The voice kept repeating itself, calm and polite, like whoever was on the other end wasn't living in a world where mutant dingos could steal your shoes.

Cooper tapped the radio.

"Uh… hello?"

Static.

He tapped it again.

"This is Cooper. I guess. Who's out there?"

The radio crackled. "Mayday, anyone out there. Please need help."

Cooper's eyes narrowed.

"Well, that's just rude. I'm trying to talk to you."

He fiddled with the knobs before the voice came through clearer.

"Please… anyone… out there… we're trapped… Vault 19… need supplies… coordinates… 23.105, -109.432."

Cooper's brain took a full five seconds to register the word "supplies."

His stomach growled.

He couldn't remember the last time he ate something that didn't taste like burnt rubber and sadness.

Vaults were old Australian government bunkers sealed off before everything went kaboom. If someone was calling from inside one.

The bunker might have food.

Actual food.

Canned beans. Vegemite. Maybe even the holy grail of wasteland cuisine: a hot-cross bun.

Cooper's survival instincts kicked in.

He grabbed his gear, a backpack full of miscellaneous crap, half a crowbar, and a Swiss Army knife, missing all the useful parts. Then he set off toward the coordinates like a man on a mission.

It took him two days to reach the site, mostly because he got lost trying to follow his own hand-drawn map.

Vault 19 was hidden beneath an old petrol station, buried under sand and rubble. Cooper poked around until he found a hatch with a keypad.

He pressed every button on the panel in random order.

Nothing happened.

He gave it his best intimidating glare.

Still nothing.

Finally, he tried what always worked back in the old world.

He smacked it.

The hatch creaked open with a hiss.

"See?" Cooper grinned. "High-tech security. No match for Cooper Branson."

Inside, the air was stale and smelled like expired air fresheners. Flickering emergency lights lined the narrow hallway. The place was eerily quiet except for the distant crackle of speakers still looping the distress signal.

Cooper crept forward; crowbar half-raised.

"Hello?" he called out, voice cracking slightly. "Uh, anyone alive in here?"

No answer.

He passed storage rooms filled with empty shelves, old office chairs, and filing cabinets containing absolutely zero useful information unless mutant kangaroos were into tax records.

Eventually, he found the source of the signal: a busted-up radio console in what looked like a security office. The same message played on repeat from a cracked speaker.

Cooper stared.

"Wait a second…"

He leaned in and saw that there was dust on the microphone. The chair behind the desk was tipped over. A rat skeleton lay curled up in one corner, looking mildly disappointed by the lack of snacks.

It finally hit him.

The distress signal had been running on autopilot for decades.

No survivors.

No supplies.

No hot-cross buns.

Cooper slumped into the chair, groaning loud enough to echo down the hall.

"All that walking for a haunted radio."

He glanced around the room, half-hoping a secret snack cabinet would reveal itself out of pity.

Nothing.

He leaned forward and pressed the microphone button out of sheer spite.

"This is Cooper. Mayday. Please send I don't know tacos. Over."

Static.

He sighed.

Then, faint through the crackling speaker, Cooper heard.

"Tacos? Over."

Cooper's heart nearly stopped.

He scrambled forward, smacking the button again.

"Wait, what? Hello? Did you say tacos?"

"No. Just messing with you. Over."

Cooper's eye twitched.

The apocalypse was bad enough. Now the radios were sarcastic as well.

He slumped back in the chair, staring at the ceiling.

Outsmarted by a machine.

Cooper took the radio since he thought it would look nice next to the vending machine keypad. Besides, if he was going to wander the wasteland of Australia alone, he might as well have someone to talk to.

About The Author

Flung into one of life's most daunting challenges at just eleven years old, José's journey began in Havana, Cuba. The Cuban Revolution uprooted his family, forcing his parents to make a heart-wrenching decision: send him away alone to safety. José boarded a plane, uncertain of what lay ahead, and landed not in the comfort of familiar faces but at an orphanage in a small Georgia town called Washington.

For the next seven years, he navigated life as a stranger in a foreign land. Letters were few, and the hope of reuniting with his parents became a distant dream. Finally, at eighteen—now a high school graduate in Atlanta—he embraced his family once again. The reunion was bittersweet, for José had grown up without them, becoming independent far sooner than most.

Determined to carve out a life for himself, José pursued a degree in Business Administration at Georgia State University. He stepped into the world of finance, starting at First National Bank of Atlanta (now Wells Fargo). His natural talent for numbers and strategic thinking propelled him to become a project manager in financial consulting, leading high-stakes ventures. His career took him across the globe, from bustling cities in the United States to financial hubs in Europe and even the sunburnt coasts of Australia.

It was in Camden, New South Wales, that a new chapter of José's life began. While exploring the quiet rhythms of this Australian town, José stumbled upon a local writers' group. What began as a casual interest soon grew into an unquenchable passion. The stories swirling in his mind took shape, and from that creative spark, Danny Monk, his first major character, was born—a mischievous, intriguing figure who captured the complexities José had observed throughout his life. Writing Danny's story was a revelation, and with that, José discovered a new calling.

Fast forward to today. José is not just a writer but a prolific storyteller, balancing multiple projects at once. He is deep into his seventh short story collection while simultaneously crafting his latest work—a crime novel slated for release in 2026. His books, filled with engaging characters and complex narratives, reflect a life rich with experiences, challenges, and triumphs.

Yet José's world is not confined to the keyboard and screen. Inspiration comes from everywhere, and one of his favourite pastimes is to wander the local mall, quietly observing people, noting quirks, behaviours, and snippets of conversation that might spark a new character or plot twist. When he's not writing or gathering ideas, José immerses himself in literature, feeding his mind with the words of others.

Outside of his creative pursuits, José treasures the simple pleasures of life—particularly long walks with his wife, Miriam, through the scenic streets of Spring Farm. Their leisurely strolls are a cherished routine, moments of reflection where stories, memories, and dreams intertwine.

José's life is a tapestry woven from adversity, perseverance, and creativity. From the orphanage in Georgia to the financial districts of the world, and now to the quiet corners of Spring Farm, where stories are born, his journey is a testament to the resilience of the human spirit. And with each book he writes, José not only tells stories but also leaves behind pieces of himself, enriching the lives of readers across the globe.

Of course, your comments, and reviews are always welcome.

Please be sure you visit my website https://worldbookreviews.com.au/book-reviews/ and let me know what you thought of this anthology of short stories and poetry.

Good, bad, or indifferent, I welcome your honest opinion.

Thank you for your purchase!

José F. Nodar © 2026

Other books by José F. Nodar

English

- Books, Pens & Larceny
- Mending Hearts at Crystal Cove
- A Live Finally Spoken
- The Ghost Detective's First Case
- The Universe Between Us
- The Time Bus
- SEX
- The Compass Legacy
- Stories to Share with My Partner Book 1
- Stories to Share with My Partner Book 2
- Stories to Share with My Partner Book 3
- Stories to Share with My Partner Book 4
- Stories to Share with My Partner Book 5
- Stories to Share with My Partner Book 6
- Stories to Share with My Partner Book 7
- Stories to Share with My Partner Book 8

Spanish

- Cuentos Para Compartir con Mi Pareja Libro 1
- Cuentos Para Compartir con Mi Pareja Libro 2
- Cuentos Para Compartir con Mi Pareja Libro 3
- Libros, Bolígrafos y Hurto
- Reparando Corazones en Crystal Cove
- Un Amor Expresado
- El Autobús del Tiempo

www.ingramcontent.com/pod-product-compliance
Lightning Source LLC
Chambersburg PA
CBHW040517170726
48295CB00012B/241